Raymond picked up the red file that lay on the desk, 'A test to destruction,' he said, 'I really don't like the red files.'

'It'll be your last test drive for us before you retire,' said Sam, then he added, 'I wish I could afford to retire.' He was big, black, very strong and very good-natured; he was also a friend and, as a safety man, very good at his job. 'The car is prepped and waiting for you on the test track. Come on, Ray, it's the last one.'

Raymond pulled his fireproof overalls on over his fireproof underwear and picked up his crash helmet. 'Let's see what we can find,' he said as they left the office and walked to the test track.

'Looks like a nice car. It's a shame I have to destroy it.' He opened the door and slid into the driver's seat. His seat belts were pulled very tight and secured by the safety team, then they shut the door and he was alone. This was the part he didn't like; what seemed an eternity passed and then the radio in his crash helmet came to life.

'Ray, you can start the engine.' Raymond turned the ignition on and pressed the start button. When he was sure all the warning lights were off and all the gauges were giving a reading he said, 'Everything looks good to go.'

'Take it out for a few laps, make sure no warning

lights come on,' said the voice inside his crash helmet. This was not new to Raymond for he had worked for Sam as a test driver for many years.

'Acknowledged,' he replied. He moved away and slowly began to increase the speed. 'Everything looks good,' he reported. 'I'll allow it to come to normal operating temperature, and get used to the way it handles before we try anything.' After ten laps the voice in his helmet spoke again, 'Ray, now the test begins, all the telemetry looks good with us, is there anything abnormal that you can feel or see?'

'Everything looks and feels good.'

'Acknowledged. You can increase the speed in your own time.' Raymond started to put the new prototype under more pressure, for the next five laps he began testing to find the car's limit.

'It performs well, everything still looking good,' he reported. Then the instruction that he didn't want to hear came through the radio.

'Ray, next time on the fast straight take it to maximum speed and try to turn it over on the curve. Your safety team will be there if you need them.'

'Acknowledged,' he replied. The radio went silent and Raymond pushed his foot to the floor. The prototype was very quick and stable, he watched the speed increasing and the RPM rising, almost entering the red zone. At the end of the straight he was travelling at the maximum speed the vehicle was capable of. Then he jerked the steering wheel suddenly, encouraging the car to become unstable as it turned into the curve.

The back wheels started to lose adhesion to the track as he deliberately took the curve far too fast and, just to help it along, he touched the kerb with the right

The
Man
with the
Flintlock Pistols

David Lawrence

Auxillium Press

British Library Cataloguing in Publication Data.
A catalogue record for this book is available
from the British Library.

Published in the United Kingdom by Auxillium Press,
an assisted publishing imprint of
Wordcatcher Publishing Group Ltd
www.wordcatcher.com
Tel: 02921 888321
Facebook.com/WordcatcherPublishing

First Edition: 2019
Print edition ISBN: 9781911265948
Ebook edition ISBN: 9781789422481
Crime

front tyre. That started to lift the car, and as if that wasn't enough he jabbed the brakes, sending a lot of stored energy through the body of the prototype making it vibrate as it launched itself into the air.

The impact on landing caused the windscreen to fragment, but it remained in place. A sequence of rolls followed, and then the fire started. The fuel cap had opened and the sparks from the metal body had ignited it; the car eventually ended its journey of destruction coming to rest, upside down, flames licking around the back wheels.

Raymond switched off the ignition and hit the central button of his seat belt. The five-point harness released him from his seat, but this resulted in him falling onto the roof and landing on his head. Even with the crash helmet on, he was dazed. Then there were flames all around him and he feared that he might be burned alive. He felt a surge of adrenalin as he struggled to open the door to escape.

The already broken windscreen suddenly shattered and two very strong, gloved hands reached in and gripped the handles on the shoulders of his overalls. He was aware of being dragged out of the car through the broken windscreen and lying on the grass beside the test track. Slowly he regained his senses and, undoing the fastenings of his crash helmet, he took it off.

'Sam,' he said, 'that was a close one. Thank you for being here, again. You saved my life.'

'Only a small percentage burst into flames, fire is a rare occurrence with these new cars,' said his friend. This was not the first time Sam had pulled Raymond from a prototype car that was being tested to destruction, and Raymond knew he owed his life to

Sam many times over, but it was the nature of the work.

'There'll be no more red files for me.' Raymond sat up and surveyed the remains of the car he had destroyed. 'Look, the fuel cap cover has been ripped off in the crash. The report will advise modification to the fuel cap, leakage of fuel was the cause of the fire.' Raymond and Sam watched as the safety team extinguished the last remaining flames. Then Sam helped Raymond to his feet and they walked slowly back to the office.

While Raymond removed his fireproof overalls, exchanging them for his corduroy jacket and trousers, he said, 'That car was one of the best, everything worked well, except for the fire, but we can give the manufacturers the answers to that problem.'

'That's what I like to hear.' said Sam, 'Your last test was a success, even if you did destroy the car. I'll give them the go ahead, with a modification to the fuel cap.'

'We have had some scary adventures, but now I've officially retired.' Raymond made his way to the door and, as he opened it, the safety team, his friends, were waiting outside for him.

'Don't forget us, Ray,' they called to him.

'I won't, I'll see you all at the party at my house tonight. The Five Pines. There will be plenty to drink.'

'I hope you won't forget me either,' said Sam.

'Sam, I'll never forget you. I know it was for work, but you looked death in the face every time you pulled me from a test to destruction. You know vehicles that take the kind of impact we put on them are very unpredictable in the first seconds of coming to rest.'

'You mean the impact that you put on them.'

'You know, and so do I, that this kind of work creates a bond,' Raymond tapped Sam on his shoulder, then took his hand. He looked into his friend's eyes, 'you'll always be my friend, Sam.' He knew he owed Sam so much more than he could say. Sam also felt something as he took Raymond's hand, he knew that here was a friend for life.

'Call in any time.' Both men released their grip. 'I might be able to find something for you to test.' Raymond hadn't given much thought as to what he was going to do now that he didn't have to work for a living, but one thing he did know, he would miss Sam.

'Thanks Sam, I'll see you this evening at my house. My days of danger and excitement are over; but I'll still never forget you and the team.'

'I will look forward to seeing this mansion that you have inherited. See you tonight.' Raymond walked across the car park and left in his new Ferrari.

Dusk had fallen when Sam and the safety team arrived at Raymond's house. He had ordered a lot of beer and whisky that had been delivered that afternoon. He welcomed his friends and they talked of all the dangers and good times that they had shared together. They drank to each other's health, a lot, and then they started on the whisky. The lounge was Raymond's favourite room in the house, it was on the second floor and had a big bay window that looked out over the drive and turning circle.

Sam and Raymond left the team on the ground floor and they retired to the lounge. They talked for a long time and, as the evening wore on, they would hear a few of the team shout, 'Thanks for the drinks, good night, Ray.' After two or three interruptions like this, Sam said, 'I must be leaving you. It sounds as though the rest of the men have left and are lost somewhere in the grounds.'

Raymond saw Sam to the big oak front door, they shook hands and Sam went in search of his team, Raymond returned to the lounge. He sat on the very large settee and looked at the glowing log fire, a smile came to his face as he listened to Sam and his men singing somewhere in the grounds of the stately house.

2

Raymond Spade lived alone on Exmoor. The house, The Five Pines, together with a substantial fortune had been bequeathed to him by his aunt, who had been one of his last remaining relatives. Now, there was just him and a cousin, Richard, who lived in Switzerland. Raymond was about 5' 10 with dark hair and hazel coloured eyes, in his early thirty's. Tonight he had swapped his casual clothes for an evening suit.

Thanks to his aunt's generous Will, he'd been able to retire from being a test driver but he hadn't expected the taste for danger or a quest for adventure, to be still very much alive within him. When Raymond moved into The Five Pines, he couldn't know what fate had in store for him.

After an evening at the theatre, Raymond and his very good friend, Francesca Sommers, were driving home. It was a clear night,a very bright moon and lots of stars lit up the dark sky.

Francesca was of medium build with dark shoulder-length hair and dark brown eyes. Tonight, she was wearing a black evening gown with a slim silver belt at her waist. She lived with her father near Dunster, where she spent a lot of her time helping him with his work.

They had left the town of Minehead and were travelling through the country roads towards Dunster. It was the early hours of the morning when the red Ferrari arrived at the little cottage. It was painted white with black old oak beams; its location was about half a mile from Dunster.

Mr. Sommers had waited up for his daughter. He knew that she had spent the evening at the theatre with Raymond and so he was not concerned; for he knew him well. They had met about two months previously in Austria. It must have been serendipity that they had been staying at the same inn.

* * *

Raymond was taking a holiday in a traditional inn he had heard about through friends. It was surrounded by charming woodlands, there was also an old castle and beer garden nearby. He'd heard the local legends of vampires and werewolves, and thought it would be interesting to investigate them, but his attention was drawn to Mr. Sommers and his daughter who were staying at the same inn. Mr. Sommers was there to deliver a lecture on advanced technical electronics with regard to alarm systems used in the museums and jewellers in Vienna. He was on a tour, having also given lectures in Paris, Rome and London.

Raymond knew there was something about Francesca as soon as he saw her and he was very swift to make her acquaintance. While Mr. Sommers was delivering his lectures, they spent a day or two together enjoying the beautiful countryside just outside Vienna. Then one evening at the inn, she introduced him to her father.

'I would like you to meet Raymond Spade.'

Mr. Sommers held out his hand, 'I'm pleased to make your acquaintance Mr. Spade.'

'And I yours,' answered Raymond.

'Ray lives not far from us,' said Francesca, 'in one of the big houses in its own grounds on Exmoor.'

'What a coincidence this is, we live so close to

each other and we have had to come to Austria to meet,' said Mr. Sommers.

'Yes, that is the long way around,' Raymond said with a smile.

'Will you join us for dinner?'

'I would be pleased to, thank you,'

'Tell me, my boy, what is it you do for a living?'

'Oh, he's retired,' answered Francesca.

'I tested prototype vehicles before they went into production,' Raymond added.

'I am not as fortunate as you, Mr. Spade, I'm not due to retire for another two months.'

'Please, call me Ray.'

'Very well, Ray it shall be.'

That evening had been very pleasant and after a beautiful meal they sat in the lounge talking and drinking brandy until it was late. Francesca was the first to retire, bidding first her father and then Raymond goodnight. They watched her as she made her way across the lounge and then she was lost from their sight.

'She's a good girl; she has come on this trip with me because she knows I forget things like my notes when I give these lectures. She makes sure we are on the right trains and planes. I would be lost without her. When this series of lectures is completed, I will retire.'

'Retirement will be good for you, it will allow you to do everything that you don't have time for,' Raymond said with a smile.

'It seems to be good for you, my boy,' stated Mr. Sommers as he rose from his chair, 'I think I will take a stroll in the garden before I retire to bed, so I will bid you goodnight.'

'Goodnight Sir, sleep well.'

The following morning Raymond was awakened by cries for help and a commotion from downstairs. He swiftly dressed himself and went to investigate. The scene that met his eyes as he entered the lounge was a strange one. A rather large man, with a thick black bushy moustache and a full head of black hair was standing in the middle of the room, dishevelled-looking and obviously very agitated. Raymond estimated him to be in his mid-fifties. His name was Klaus Inman.

The landlord of the inn guided him to a comfortable chair and settled him down. Then he asked, 'What has happened? You look like you need a brandy.'

Klaus was very frightened and his voice fluttered as he tried to explain what he had seen. 'It was last night,' he said, 'I was walking back to the inn through the wooded area from the beer garden. There was a full moon and I could see my way quite clearly. I was just passing the fork in the path that leads to the old castle when I saw a man; at least I think it was a man. He was dressed in black with a long black cloak that had a red silk lining on the inside. He was forcing an older man along the other path towards the castle.

When he saw me, he beckoned me to follow them, when I refused, he started to approach me. He had two long silver points protruding from his hand. I tried to run but, in my panic, I tripped over something and struck my head. It was dawn when I awoke. The beer garden isn't far from here and the old castle is even closer,' then he whispered, 'I have heard stories about the old castle, it is home to vampires, werewolves and ghosts. The castle is not a place to be, especially at night.'

'How much did you have to drink last night, Klaus?' asked the landlord.

'Not many; two or three beers, and a whisky chaser for each beer,' he answered.

'With the amount of alcohol you consumed, it's a wonder you didn't see pink elephants last night,' said the landlord as he left to continue his morning duties that kept the inn functioning smoothly.

The small crowd that had gathered around to listen to Klaus, laughed amongst themselves and began slowly dispersing, each one making their own witticism as they left. Klaus sat back in the comfortable chair and as the last of the people moved away, he found himself alone, but safe and he was glad of that.

Raymond had listened to Klaus's story and was just about to approach the portly man when someone called his name. It was Francesca, she looked worried.

'Ray, have you seen my father?'

'Not since last night, he said he was going to take a stroll around the garden before retiring for the night.'

'His bed hasn't been slept in,' she said anxiously, 'it's not like him to leave without saying anything.'

'Try not to worry Fran, we'll find him.' He led Francesca to a small table and waited until he was sure that she was comfortably seated in one of the chairs, 'Order some coffee,' he said, 'I must speak to Klaus for a moment.' He left her and crossed the room to where Klaus was sitting.

'Klaus,' he said softly. The man looked up at him. 'I am sorry, I don't know your surname, mine is Spade

11

and I would like to talk to you about what you saw last night.'

'Mine is Inman, Klaus Inman and I would like to talk to someone who would believe me.' He started to rise from the chair as he introduced himself offering his hand as he did. Raymond took it and they both sat down.

'I came to stay at this inn because I heard the stories about vampires and werewolves. I heard what you told the others just now, but can you give me a description of the older man?'

'Let me see,' he paused, 'he was tall, with grey hair and thin. He was wearing a black suit,' he paused again, 'yes, he was wearing a black suit.'

'Mr. Inman...'

'Klaus,' the portly man corrected him.

'Very well, Klaus, I think this man might be a friend of mine. Will you take me to the place where you saw them last night?'

Klaus hesitated for a moment before answering. 'If that is what you want, certainly I will.'

'Wait here for me, Klaus, I'll be right back.' He rose from his chair and crossed the lounge to where he had left Francesca waiting.

'Fran, I have to go out with Klaus, I should be back by lunchtime. Will you stay here? Wait for me?'

Fran fiddled anxiously with her coffee cup. 'Ok, I'll wait here in case my father comes back. Till lunchtime,' she watched Raymond and Klaus leave the lounge.

It was a warm sunny morning, just right for an enjoyable walk and Raymond would have welcomed it, if he hadn't had thoughts of a rescue flowing through his mind. They walked along the footpath towards the beer garden and it wasn't long before they reached the fork in the path.

'Just here,' said Klaus. He began to explain the happenings of the evening. 'This path leads to the beer garden and it was along that one that I saw the two men. It leads to the old castle.' He shuddered at the thought of what had happened.

'Shall we take a look at the castle?' asked Raymond. Reluctantly Klaus agreed. Together they walked on. The path was now more like a tunnel as the woodland became thick on both sides of them. They walked on until the undergrowth subsided into fields and the castle became visible to them. It looked deserted.

'Do you think that the older man was brought here?'

'This path only leads to the castle,' answered Klaus.

'It all looks deserted now,' remarked Raymond, 'let's go back to the inn. Thanks for showing me the castle. I'll buy you a beer when we get back.'

'I'll hold you to that, Mr. Spade,' said Klaus not being a man to ever refuse a drink.

'Klaus, the name is Ray.'

'I will hold you to that, Ray.' The two men turned their backs on the castle and entered the woodland. As they approached the fork in the footpath, they heard voices. One was a man's, the other a girl's, and she sounded quite distressed.

'You will come with me or you will meet your death here!'

The girl began to scream. Raymond left Klaus and ran along the path to where it forked. As he arrived he saw a man dressed in a black suit with a black cloak around his shoulders dragging a girl along the path.

'You will come with me!' he shouted.

Raymond was blocking the path that led to the old castle when Klaus caught up behind him, trying to catch his breath. As the man in black continued to pull the girl along the path, he suddenly caught sight of the men standing in front of him. He stopped pulling the girl. 'You better get out of my way if you know what is good for you.'

Raymond recognised the girl, how could he not, for it was Francesca. When she realised that the man confronting her kidnapper was Raymond, she stopped struggling.

'Are you hurt?'

'Not yet,' she replied. Raymond looked into the eyes of his opponent, 'You are not going to take her with you,' he said calmly. The man flung Francesca to the ground.

'Do you think you can stop me?' he said menacingly. He took what looked like a silver knuckleduster out of his pocket. It had two sharp points protruding from it and he fitted it to his right hand. Raymond knew the damage it could do.

'Come on, little man, you can't hope to survive a conflict with a vampire. Come to your death.'

By now Klaus had stopped panting and was standing next to Raymond.

'That's it, Mr. Spade, just like I said, it's a vampire.'

'If it is, it should be in its coffin, not out in the morning sunshine.'

'I can't fight with that thing, Mr. Spade, I am sorry,' the portly man made a run for it. 'I hope I will see you back at the inn!' he shouted as he ran towards the beer garden.

'Just you and me,' said the vampire, 'come to me, little man. Come and meet your doom.' He checked that the deadly knuckle duster was fitted tightly on to his hand; he pushed his black cloak over his shoulders and walked menacingly towards Raymond. He knew Francesca could not escape for to do so she would have to pass him. If she followed the path in the other direction it would only lead her to the old castle.

Raymond breathed deeply, and slowly walked towards his opponent, for that was all he was as far as Raymond was concerned. His mind was clear, his gaze flowed over his target like moonlight, ready to react to any sudden movement and strike at any vulnerable pressure point.

The figure in black lunged at Raymond once and then again, with the shining pronged knuckleduster, but Raymond side stepped the first angry attempt and, as the second flashed past his ear, he brought his foot up and hit his foe low in the stomach.

The kick winded his opponent, but just then Raymond saw Francesca move and, for a split second, he lost his concentration. The knuckleduster smashed into his left shoulder, the prongs causing tremendous pain in his bicep. The shock left him numb and the force of the blow sent him to his knees. His attacker's left fist struck his right temple and sent him sprawling face down onto the dusty footpath, where he lay unconscious.

It was late afternoon when Raymond regained his senses, his left arm was numb and his shirt was soaked with blood. He dragged himself to his feet and though feeling dizzy, he started to walk back to the inn. This took some time. He didn't meet anyone and so he had no assistance to get back.

When he reached the inn, he found the landlord and asked him to find some bandages. The landlord said, 'Shall I ask a doctor to take a look at your arm? It looks quite bad.'

'Thank you,' Raymond replied, 'it's not as bad as it looks.'

'I will send one of the maids with a first aid kit right away if you are sure that is all you will need.' Raymond started to make his way to his room and as though it was an afterthought he said, 'Would you ask room service to send a meal in about half an hour.'

'Certainly, Mr. Spade,' replied the landlord.

When he reached his room, he waited not removing any clothing until there was a knock on his door. He opened it to see a young girl holding a tray with a selection of new, unwrapped bandages on it.

'The landlord said he hoped that these would meet your requirements, Sir,' Raymond took three of the bandages.

'Will that be all, Sir?' she asked.

'Yes, thank you,' Raymond replied and shut the door. Now that he was alone, he very slowly removed his jacket and shirt. There was a large, dark bruise on his bicep and two holes that were still oozing blood. With the use of a flannel, warm water and a big bath towel he managed to clean up and bandage his wounds. After he had changed his clothes and enjoyed the meal that had been sent to his room he was ready to leave. Just before he did, he found the landlord.

'I'm sorry for the mess that your staff will find in

my room, I may have damaged some of the things in the bathroom,' he explained.

'I am sure we can replace any bathroom items. I trust that you are not too badly injured?' inquired the Landlord.

'No, nothing serious,' answered Raymond, 'but now I have to go out.' Just as he was leaving the inn, he met Klaus Inman coming in. Klaus grabbed Raymond by the shoulders; a searing pain shot through his left arm.

'Thank God you are alright!'

Raymond removed Klaus's hand from his injured shoulder. Then he guided him between the tables and made the wobbly man comfortable in one of the large chairs. The landlord, seeing what was happening crossed the dining room and positioned himself close to the drunken man.

'Where have you been?' Raymond asked.

'Where have I been?' repeated Klaus, 'Oh yes, I remember. I have been in the beer garden.'

'You've hit the bottle hard this time, haven't you?'

'It was mostly beer,' Klaus corrected him. Then he asked, 'What happened to the vampire?'

'He escaped, but don't worry about him. Have that drink I promised you. One more or less won't make any difference to your condition.'

'Are you suggesting that I'm inebriated?'

'That is a big word on such a lot of alcohol.'

'Yes, it is, isn't it, and you're right, I am drunk.'

'Klaus, listen to me. I am going back to the old castle…' The portly man interrupted him, 'You must be mad!' he cried.

'Klaus, listen to me,' he persisted, 'if I have not

returned by dawn, tell the landlord where I have gone and ask him to notify the police. You lead them to the old castle.'

'Alright, Ray, it's the least I can do after leaving you this morning,' he settled back into the chair. As Raymond turned to leave the landlord said, 'I wasn't trying to overhear your conversation but I did hear enough to know what you want me to do, if you are not back by dawn.'

'Thank you,' said Raymond, 'I would prefer not to involve the police as they may delay our return home, you know, statements, withholding passports, that kind of thing. Will you give Klaus whatever he wants? I'll settle his bill.'

'Certainly, Mr. Spade,' the landlord replied.

Raymond left the inn as dusk fell and walked purposefully along the dusty path between the trees until he reached the fork in the path. To his left lay the beer garden, to his right the old castle. He looked up at the sky, the stars were shining in the heavens and the moon was bright. He had brought a small torch with him, but it was not necessary. He continued along the path that led to the old castle.

'What superstitions the night brings,' he thought, 'werewolves, vampires. The night makes everything...' he paused for a moment, '...different.'

He considered himself foolhardy to try to rescue Francesca from a place he didn't know and from a foe who had already beaten him once.

'A vampire,' he said aloud. 'Klaus is right, I must be mad, but this is personal and how can I live with myself if I don't try?' He entered the path with the overhanging trees, it was quite dark but he still didn't use his torch. Anyone in the castle may see the light and that was the last thing he wanted. The element of surprise was the only advantage he had. He moved cautiously, the crickets or grasshoppers were chirruping in the grass and a bat narrowly missed flying into him.

'Very appropriate,' he said.

3

At last he was standing outside the old castle. There were signs in German that he assumed warned sightseers to stay out. The writing in red couldn't be anything but a warning as the castle really was a ruin. He cautiously entered staying close to the walls, in the shadows.

Looking around him; the moon was full and shone brightly, allowing him to see clearly. Across the courtyard, at the base of one of the towers was an open door.

'Carelessness, or a trap?' he said as he sprinted silently across the courtyard and entered the tower. It was dark so he reached into his pocket for his torch, its beam revealed stone steps that led up the tower, and also down below ground level. He chose to go up and climbed the steps quickly and silently.

At the top there was a door, he opened it slowly and it revealed a long passage, in darkness. The beam from his torch showed torch holders along the walls that would have provided fiery light in days gone by. He ran the length of the passage silently and with hardly any effort. At the end of the passage was a door, it was open, he entered and found himself in a large dining room illuminated by candles. The light from the dancing flames of the log fire cast shadows onto the walls like ghostly figures. There was a dark-haired girl sitting in one of the large chairs near the fire.

Now that Raymond had entered the room, he closed the door quietly behind him and crossed the room to the log fire just as noiselessly. As he approached, he could see that the girl's wrists were tied to the arms of the chair.

'Don't make a sound,' he whispered, 'I'll have you free in a moment.' He reached for the little pocket knife he always carried and opened one of the blades, its razor edge sliced through the ropes with no resistance.

'Fran,' he whispered, 'is your father here?' He replaced the knife into his pocket.

'Yes, I think he is in one of the dungeons and there are at least two other men besides the one that brought me here. I was so frightened when you didn't get up after confronting him this afternoon, and then I realised that you weren't coming after me.'

'He caught me with a lucky punch; he won't get another chance like that. Stay here and wait for me.'

'Where are you going?'

'To find your father.' Just then the door opened and a well-built, bald-headed, rugged-looking man entered.

'Come on, my pretty, you're wanted in the dungeon.'

Then the man saw Raymond.

'Who are you?' he shouted. Not giving Raymond time to answer, he advanced towards him in a menacing manner. Raymond side-stepped him and pushed him back into the big oak dining table. The man rose to his feet and attacked again. Raymond reached into his pocket for his torch and as the man approached, he aimed and threw the light with all his might. The small torch hit the man hard between the eyes and he fell to the floor, motionless.

'Keep an eye on him, Fran, if he starts to wake up, hit him on the head with a chair or something. I won't be long, I promise.' He picked up his torch and replaced it in his pocket. Francesca watched as he crossed the room and vanished from her sight.

The dungeons were dark, dismal and very damp. Raymond had no difficulty in finding the right one. The door was open and it was light inside, there was a lot of noise. Mr. Sommers was sitting in a chair in the centre of the floor, in front of him there was a large bowl made of netted steel. It was full of red-hot coals and there were two pokers being heated in it, Raymond shuddered to think why. The man with the black suit and cloak was still shouting all kinds of threats at the old man.

'You will give us the code numbers we want or your daughter will feel a touch from these irons!' he shouted. The old man shook his head; this made his aggressor fly into a rage. He pulled one of the pokers from the red-hot coals and swung it wildly in the air.

'I have sent a man to bring your daughter here! You will soon tell us what we want to know!'

'Code numbers are for identification, they won't switch off an alarm system.'

Raymond knew he had to do something before Mr. Sommers was hurt, so he entered the dungeon.

'We meet again,' Raymond said loudly. The man stopped swinging the red-hot poker around and looked at him.

'Tell me; are you a vampire, or just a mad man?' The man turned quickly to face Raymond. Then without warning he threw the poker at him. The man was so angry that his aim was way off, Raymond barely had to move for the poker to miss him; it hit the wall behind him with a crash.

'If that is the best you can do, I don't fancy your

chances,' Raymond said in a bid to further annoy his opponent.

Then the vampire-man leapt into the air and sent a punch into Raymond's left shoulder. It knocked him off his feet and opened the wounds under the bandages; his left arm was now almost useless. He was surprised that his enemy had remembered his injury from their last encounter.

'Don't underestimate him again,' he thought to himself as he rose to his feet. His opponent came at him again, his foot missed its target but his left fist found its mark as it crashed into Raymond's right cheekbone. He felt a sickening dizziness and he knew he would soon only be semi-conscious. He was aware of the punches raining in around his head and the occasional stabbing pain in his left shoulder. He tried to defend himself with his right hand, but to no avail. His left arm was wet, What damage the vampire had done he dare not think.

Raymond had managed to hit his adversary once or twice around his throat and neck and, even though he had hit the right pressure points, they were not hard enough to cause any damage. Finally, a devastating right fist sent him sprawling across the stone floor and he came to rest next to the bowl of hot coals. Raymond saw the vampire take a shiny object from his pocket and, as he pushed it onto his hand, he realised it was the knuckleduster.

The vampire ran and dived into the air, trying to kill Raymond by sinking the deadly points of the weapon into his neck. Raymond had to do something quickly. He reached for the other poker that was still being heated. It was hot to touch but he gripped it tightly and pulled it from the coals.

The vampire was coming at him at such a speed that he couldn't save himself, when he saw Raymond holding the red-hot iron he tried to avoid its glowing tip. Raymond aimed it at the ferocious figure and it sliced into him, piercing him just to the side of his stomach. The vampire staggered back and pulled the poker out, burning his hand as he did. There was no blood. Raymond realised the hot poker must have cauterised the wound. The vampire pulled his black cloak around him and staggered out of the dungeon.

Raymond pulled himself to his feet and asked, 'Are you hurt, Mr. Sommers?'

'No, I'm alright,' he replied. 'You don't look so good though.'

'Francesca is waiting for us upstairs,' said Raymond, 'she'll be glad to see you.'

'She will be glad to see you too, my boy.' They turned to leave the dungeons, when to their surprise they heard a voice.

'Surely you are not leaving.' They turned to see a man stepping out of the shadows of the dungeon walls. He had been listening to the interrogation. He had a full head of grey hair and was wearing a grey trench coat that was open at the front. Under his coat was a dark green velvet jacket and a dark blue waist coat that was sporting a gold watch chain. But the most interesting thing was the jewel encrusted flintlock duelling pistol that he was pointing at them.

'I don't know you, do I?' asked Raymond.

'Neither of you know me, but I know about you, Mr. Sommers. My name is Louis La Ronde and my name should strike fear into the people who know me,' he boasted, 'and that was Victor the Vampire who just left us. I think he may hold a grudge after that encounter with you, Mr. Spade,' he walked slowly towards them.

'You know my name.'

'I did some checking up on you after your encounter with Victor this morning. You used to be a test driver, but now you are retired. This is the second time you have tried to interfere in my plans. I am known in the circles that I frequent as the Second-Hand Man, I own a shop called the Second-Hand Antique Shop; I deal in secondhand merchandise. I obtain objects, any object, for a price. Currently I am in search of the Snowflake Diamond.' He spoke with a French accent.

'I have never heard of the Snowflake Diamond,' stated Raymond.

'I believe you, Mr. Spade, but you have, haven't you Mr. Sommers?'

'Is that what all this is about? Yes, I have heard of it, but I don't have it,' he said.

'No, you don't have it, but it is protected by the alarm systems that you know so much about. All I want from you is a list of code numbers from the newest systems,' he stated.

'As I told your vampire friend, you can't switch an alarm off using code numbers. The code number is just for identification.'

Then Louis La Ronde realised that Mr. Sommers may know code numbers but he didn't know combinations that could be changed every twenty-four hours. He would have to find another way to obtain the Snowflake Diamond. Quite abruptly he said, 'Gentlemen, I must take my leave.'

He walked to the door, 'I am sure I need not tell you; speak not a word to anyone of my involvement in

25

this unfortunate turn of events. As I said, those that know me know enough to fear me. I have found you once, I can find you again.' He replaced the flintlock pistol under his trench coat and then he was gone.

'He is a bit theatrical, don't you think?' Raymond said as he and Mr. Sommers left the dungeon and walked slowly back to the dining room. When they entered Francesca flung her arms around her father, 'Oh, I am so glad you're alright.'

Raymond looked around the room and said 'Where is the other man?'

'After you left, he regained consciousness and ran away shouting some threats, that we won't get away with this, whatever this is,' she replied.

Raymond crossed the room and looked out of the window. It was still dark.

'We should start back to the inn, I asked the landlord to contact the police if I wasn't back by dawn.' Francesca moved close to Raymond and whispered, 'Thank you, Ray, I don't know what would have happened if you hadn't been here to help us.'

She put her arms around him and kissed him softly on the cheek. When she drew away from him, her right hand was wet. She looked at it and then at Raymond.

'It's blood,' she whispered.

'Yes,' he replied.

'Are you hurt?' she asked.

'It's just my shoulder, it will heal. But now we must go.'

Mr. Sommers, Francesca and Raymond left the old castle, never to return.

The walk back to the inn was very pleasant and the early morning air helped to make the terrible events of that night feel unreal and far away. When they reached the inn, Mr. Sommers and Francesca went to their rooms. Raymond went into the lounge bar and there, sleeping in a comfortable chair in the corner, was Klaus Inman.

The landlord heard Raymond and his friends enter the inn and came to meet them. He entered the bar and greeted Raymond.

'Good morning.'

'Good morning,' Raymond replied, 'what's happened to Klaus?'

'I made him comfortable and gave him some brandy. He drank a few glasses and talked about vampires and then passed out.'

'Vampires,' repeated Raymond, 'they don't exist,' he said with a smile.

He gave the landlord a friendly tap on the back, and there is no need to disturb the police at this early hour,' he left him with Klaus and went up to his room.

A week later, Raymond, Mr. Sommers and Francesca returned to England and Raymond began to spend more time with Francesca.

* * *

It was the early hours of the morning when the Ferrari stopped on the driveway of the little cottage. Raymond switched off the engine of the sleek sports car and, as he did, the front door was opened by Francesca's father.

'Raymond,' he called.

'That's unusual,' Francesca puzzled, 'I wonder what's wrong?' Raymond helped Francesca from the car and they entered the cottage, closing the front door behind them.

'Ray, my boy; I have something I would like you to see.' He handed Raymond an envelope.

'It's an invitation to an evening at the Second-Hand Antique Shop in London. Tomorrow night.'

'Louis La Ronde's Antique Shop?' asked Raymond.

'Yes. I thought we were finished with him.'

'I thought so too,' stated Raymond.

'Is this to do with that diamond he was going to steal?' asked Francesca.

'Maybe,' Raymond answered as he placed the envelope inside his jacket.

Two months had passed since the vampire incident and Mr. Sommers had now retired. He was glad to have put all that horror behind him.

'Leave this invitation with me.' Raymond reassured them. He looked at his friends and said, 'I won't let anything happen to either of you.' Then he turned to leave, 'Don't worry, I'll see you after I have sorted this out.'

They watched as Raymond reversed the Ferrari out of the driveway and vanished into the night.

Raymond had not made any specific plan for his visit to London, but he had checked to see exactly where the Second-Hand Antique Shop was and had decided to park his Ferrari about a block away. It was early in the evening when Raymond pushed open the door and entered the shop. He was met by a well-built, well-dressed man with a bald head.

'Good evening,' he said, 'Mr. La Ronde knew you would come.' The bald-headed man allowed Raymond to pass him and then closed the door and hung a sign on it marked 'Closed'.

'Not an open evening then,' he said. The bald-headed man gestured to Raymond to move to the back of the shop and to pass through the partially closed curtains. He made his way through the darkened shop, passing what he estimated as thousands of pounds worth of antiques.

'Go on through the curtains,' He parted them so that he could see what lay behind them. He was confronted with a dark passage and a flight of stairs.

'Go on, Spade,' encouraged the bald-headed man. Raymond walked on until he reached the stairs; these he climbed without being asked. When he reached the top, there was a door.

'Go on, open it.'

This Raymond did, but very slowly. Then he turned to the bald-headed man and said, 'After you.'

'Go in, before I lose my temper,' was the reply he received.

4

Raymond entered into a penthouse suite-come-office, he looked around. It was decorated with all kinds of antiques and included a settee with two large armchairs. There were curtains hanging on one of the walls, but they were drawn so Raymond had no clue as to what lay beyond them. Then he looked at Louis La Ronde, sitting behind a very big wooden desk. The first time Raymond had met him he was impressed with his clothes and this time was no exception; a lace cravat with a clear crystal pin, and a dark blue silk waistcoat with a gold watch chain.

'You never cease to impress me, Mr. La Ronde.'

'Or you, me. I knew you would come in your friend's place. It was you I really wanted to see, but I knew you would not oblige if I had made the invitation to you.'

Then Raymond dispensed with the pleasantries and said, 'All right, La Ronde, what do you want?'

'You know I work for anyone who wants anything. I have a client who wants the Snowflake Diamond, I will get it for him and it will be very, very expensive.'

'What has this to do with me?'

'I saw what happened in Austria. You are a formidable opponent and, as they say, I would rather have you with me than against me.'

'No,' said Raymond, 'I am not going to help you steal a diamond.'

'It isn't just a diamond, it is the Snowflake Diamond. I will pay you well.'

Raymond shook his head, 'No,' he said.

'All right, if that is your decision.' He signalled to the bald-headed man, who produced a gun from his jacket.

'Take him somewhere and shoot him.' The bald-headed man looked at Raymond.

'This way,' he said.

'La Ronde,' Raymond called, 'what about Mr. Sommers and his daughter?'

'I will have them killed too,' he replied, 'Don't want to leave any evidence around!'

'What will it take for you to leave them alone?'

'You work for me. You help me to get the Snowflake,' he answered.

Raymond stopped walking and the bald-headed man tried to move him by pushing him with his gun. Now Raymond knew exactly where the gun was, he spun around pushing the gun away with his left hand and continued to spin bringing his right hand into the side of the man's neck in a truly focused strike. As the man fell unconscious to the floor, Raymond took the gun from his hand.

'You try to harm me, or mine and I will surely kill you.'

'Don't threaten me, Spade!' snarled La Ronde.

'Do you only have the one bodyguard? Because you are going to need more than one if I come after you. What happened to the two men who were with you in Austria?'

'That's Oliver,' Louis La Ronde pointed at the bald-headed man lying at his feet. 'He was waiting to meet you again and the other is still in hospital. It was difficult trying to explain a burn like that.'

'Do you see how easily I can dispose of your men?

31

I will not tell anyone of your plan regarding the Snowflake Diamond, but I won't work for you.' Raymond walked to the large wooden desk and looked the Frenchman in the face. 'Don't make me come after you, La Ronde.' Raymond moved slowly to the door not taking his eyes off the Frenchman. He left, taking Oliver's gun with him, leaving the antique dealer, the second-hand man, with his unconscious henchman.

Raymond soon found his way out and it wasn't long before he was leaving London with its noisy traffic and congested roads. He opened up the Ferrari on the motorway, but he was pleased when he started to cross Exmoor and, at last, park his car in the driveway of The Five Pines.

He entered his house and climbed two flights of stairs, which were carpeted with a rich burgundy pile, and entered the lounge. Its decor was of wooden panels and wall-to-wall carpeting in the same rich burgundy as the staircase. Opposite the fire place was a tapestry of a wild deer. The large bay window looked over the driveway and much of the grounds. Raymond took the gun from his pocket. It was a Smith & Wesson .38 Police Special. He opened it and checked the bullets in the cylinder. There were five live rounds and one empty chamber.

'At least Oliver is a professional,' he said to himself. He closed the cylinder, lining up the empty chamber with the hammer and placed the gun on the shelf above the fireplace. He sat on the large settee and closed his eyes, just to rest them for a minute or two, but sleep engulfed him, and there he stayed.

The morning sunlight through the bay windows woke him. It was mid-morning and he had slept what was left of the night on the settee. He went to the kitchen and made himself a cup of coffee and then left the house to visit Mr. Sommers. The Ferrari wound its way through the country lanes until he arrived at the little cottage. As he approached the front door, it opened and there was Francesca, looking pale and frightened.

'What's happened?' Raymond asked.

'A man broke in about four o clock this morning and took my father away with him. I recognised him, he was the one in the castle in Austria. He said to tell you to go to the ruins of Cleeve Abbey tonight.'

Raymond took her into the cottage and closed the door.

'Ray, he wants you. Why does he want you?'

'La Ronde wants me to work for him. He thinks if I help him to steal the Snowflake Diamond, I won't bring the police down on him.'

The afternoon passed slowly but it gave Raymond time to think, and as it began to get dark he said, 'Come on, Fran, it's time to get your father back.'

They left the cottage and soon they were travelling through the country lanes to Minehead. They joined the main coast road and by-passed Dunster, eventually they reached Washford. The ruins of Cleeve Abbey lie on the outskirts of Washford about three hundred metres from the main coast road.

Raymond drove off the main road and parked his Ferrari in the car park opposite the ruined Abbey. It was dark so Raymond took the small torch that he always carried with him from his pocket.

'Come on, Fran,' he whispered. They crossed the country road and entered the grounds of the abbey.

The entrance to the Abbey passed through a two-storey gatehouse. The ground floor formed the gatehouse with a wide arch at each end. As they walked through the passage, Raymond noticed two doors. He tried the handles, but they were both locked. They walked on until they came to a large square courtyard, covered with short grass that felt like carpet under-foot. It was also surrounded on three sides by two-storey buildings. The building to their left was honeycombed with archways, but the one facing them had just three archways and some steps; it offered little protection.

Then they heard a sound behind them and turned to be confronted by two men holding guns. Mr. Sommers was between them, his hands tied behind his back. They were standing in the centre of the courtyard, about ten metres away.

'We are to make a swap, you for him,' said Oliver, the well-built one with a bald head.

'That's the man who took my father last night,' whispered Francesca.

'We have met before haven't we, Oliver?' remarked Raymond, 'I still have your gun from our last meeting.' He waited to see if there would be any reaction. There wasn't, so he added, 'Send Mr. Sommers to his daughter and I will go with you.'

He passed the keys for the Ferrari to Francesca, 'When you and your father are safe, go home and wait for me.'

One of the men kept his gun aimed at Mr. Sommers as they sent him to his daughter. Raymond walked towards them, he and Mr. Sommers passed close to each other and Raymond said, 'Don't worry, take her home; I will be back as soon as I can.'

When Mr. Sommers reached Francesca, she immediately untied her father's hands.

'Thank you my dear,' he said. As Francesca was untying her father, the two men were securing Raymond's hands behind his back.

Then one of the men said, 'I know you.' With that, he punched Raymond on his left shoulder. Raymond didn't show that his left shoulder was still tender.

'You're Victor the Vampire,' remarked Raymond, 'you must be just out of hospital, how is the burn?' he asked in an attempt to annoy the man.

Victor was about to retaliate when Oliver said, 'Fire a few shots to scare them off.'

On hearing this Raymond shouted, 'Fran! Get to the archways!' Another punch landed on Raymond's jaw. 'If you keep doing that I'm going to owe you, Victor.'

Francesca ran with her father to the honeycombed archways and found cover as the bullets began to ricochet and imbed themselves in the old buildings. They were never in any real danger as the two men were just shooting to frighten them as, by now, they couldn't see their targets. Oliver said, 'Leave them; we have what we came for! Let's go.'

The gunfire stopped and they heard Raymond being taken away.

Mr. Sommers and Francesca waited until they were sure that the two men and Raymond had gone. Then they cautiously made their way back to the car park. Francesca gave the keys for the Ferrari to her father, and once they were both in the car with their seat belts on, Mr. Sommers began to work out which switch did what.

He soon discovered how to start the car and they left Cleeve Abbey. If it hadn't been for the events of that evening, Mr. Sommers would have enjoyed

35

driving the Ferrari home. At one point he said, 'I had a sports car once, not like this one, but it was very good for its time.'

The journey didn't take long in the Ferrari and it was with a twinge of disappointment that he finally switched the engine off. Then he said, 'Raymond told me to tell you not to worry and that he would see us soon.' Francesca was out of the car first, she walked around the red sports car and proceeded to help her father out of the driver's seat.

'Not as agile as I once was,' he remarked as they went into the cottage. They closed and locked the front door behind them.

'What if they kill Ray?' Francesca asked.

'If they were going to do that, they would have killed him this evening. No, they want him to help them. They don't know who they are dealing with and, when they find out, it will be too late. Don't worry, Fran, it will take a lot to stop Ray,' he said with a smile.

5

It had been a long journey in the back of the black Mercedes, but at last it stopped. The rear door opened and Raymond was dragged out.

'Time to meet the boss, is it?' he said in a jovial manner.

'You won't be smiling when he's finished with you,' smirked Oliver.

They were back in London, outside the Second-Hand Antique Shop. They entered and Raymond was pushed between the antiques and through the curtains at the back of the shop. Then he climbed the stairs, just as he had done the last time he was here. At the top of the stairs, there was a door. Oliver opened it and Victor pushed Raymond into the room.

Behind the large desk was Louis La Ronde, this time dressed in silk shirt with lace cuffs and a cravat with a gold pin. This man had very expensive tastes.

'Mr. Spade, we meet again.'

'Not by choice.'

'No, I suppose not, but have you reconsidered working for me?'

'Why do you want me, La Ronde?'

'I know it's fruitless to try and steal the Snowflake from where it will be displayed, the job must be done whilst in transit. If I had realised that before I tried to get the alarm codes from Sommers, we would never have met. But don't you see? You are a problem. If you are with me, I can make you very rich. But if you are not, you are a significant threat.'

'I will never be with you, La Ronde.'

'Then you leave me no alternative.'

He waved at his two henchmen to come forward. They stood in front of the big desk.

'Take him away and drown him in the swimming pool.'

Oliver took Raymond by his right arm and Victor took his left and, as they walked towards the curtains that hung on the wall near La Ronde's desk, he rose and parted them. They concealed a pair of doors that looked like French windows, La Ronde opened them and together the three men left the penthouse suite-come-office and stepped out onto a rooftop patio. It was surrounded by a high wall. Raymond noticed some metal steps with hand rails about halfway along the wall that he guessed must be a fire escape.

'So, this is what the curtains were hiding,' Raymond said, his curiosity satisfied for the moment. The patio was decorated with coloured paving stones which surrounded a small swimming pool. There were easy chairs and loungers scattered around the sides of the pool with some potted plants spread around the deserted patio.

Victor checked that the rope binding Raymond's wrists was still tight then, without hesitation, he pushed him into the pool. Raymond managed to take a breath of air just before hitting the water, and then he sank. He estimated the pool to be about two meters deep.

He looked up at the surface of the water, desperately needing air. His nose and throat hurt from some of the water that he had inhaled. He knew he couldn't do this for long and so he brought his knees up to his chest and pulled his bound wrists down and around his feet. With a struggle, he managed to get his hands in front of him. He pushed off the bottom of the pool with his feet and broke through the surface of the water, dragging fresh air into his lungs. He was able to do a sort of doggy paddle that kept his head just above the water while he filled his lungs with air again. Now he was more comfortable with the situation.

Next, he felt in his pocket for the knife that he always carried. He found it, but as he tried to open the blade it fell from his hand and he watched it sink to the bottom of the pool. Filling his lungs with air he dived to retrieve it.

Oliver and Victor watched with interest as Raymond fought for his life. He was aware that his two assailants were observing him. He picked up his knife and opened the razor-sharp blade. In less than a moment he was free of his bonds. He glanced up, and yes, they were still watching him. But he needed air so he swam to the surface and hung on to the wall at the side of the pool.

When Oliver saw this, he put his foot on Raymond's head and tried to push him under the water, but Raymond was ready, he knew that they would try something so he grabbed Oliver's foot and twisted it as he pushed away from the side of the pool with all his might. The result was Oliver falling into the water close to him.

'If I can't drown you, I will choke you where you are.' He put his hands around Raymond's neck and began to squeeze. Raymond felt the blood pounding in his head and he knew he had to do something or die. He grabbed Oliver's arm and slashed his wrist with his razor-sharp knife, the blood started pumping out, discolouring the water. When Oliver realised what Raymond had done, he tried to climb out of the pool. Victor reached out to help him but Raymond saw his chance and grabbed Victors arm pulling him into the water too. Still holding Victor's arm, he pushed away from the side of the pool as he had done before. This gave him the result he wanted: both henchmen in the water while he climbed out of the pool and made his way to the metal steps.

Louis La Ronde stepped through the open doors onto the patio just in time to see his men trying to get out of the pool and Raymond standing on the fire escape.

'They may need medical assistance,' he said, then he climbed down the fire escape and vanished into the big city of London.

'Find him, bring him back here. Do you hear me? Find him!' Then he thought for a moment and his rage subsided. 'While you were trying to dispose of Mr. Spade, I have been looking for a gemmologist and I have found one. There is a Joanna Sommers; she knows about crystals, she lives on Exmoor. I suspect that she is related to the old man, Sommers. Bring her here.'

'What can we do about Spade?'

'Leave him for the moment. When we have Joanna Sommers, I am sure he will come looking for her.'

Oliver held out his left arm, his wrist was still pumping blood, 'I need help. Spade slashed my wrist,' he said with some urgency. Louis La Ronde looked at Victor and said, 'Take him to the hospital and then pick up Joanna Sommers. Her address is on my desk.'

* * *

Raymond wandered around London throughout the night. The weather was warm but he was very glad to see the morning sun. He had found a Bentley main dealer during the night and was waiting outside as the salesman arrived. Raymond went into the sales office with him, they talked for a short time and then Raymond made a phone call to a bank. He read some numbers from his bank card and left the sales man with the relevant details. 'Can I leave it to you?' he asked.

'Yes, sir,' replied the salesman. Raymond left the showroom and went to a nearby café and enjoyed a good breakfast, then he returned to the showroom.

'Is it ready?' he asked.

'Yes, sir,' answered the salesman.

'I trust there were no problems with the bank?'

'None at all,' was the reply, then a white Bentley arrived outside.

'It's been checked over and is road legal with a full tank of fuel,' explained the salesman. 'The keys are in it,' he added.

'Thank you,' said Raymond as he shook the salesman's hand and left.

He soon wound his way through the London traffic, out on to the motorway and a few hours later he was driving across Exmoor and approaching his stately house. Turning the Bentley into the driveway of The Five Pines felt right. He parked it where he usually left his Ferrari. It felt like something that he had always done.

On entering the house, he had a shower and then started to make a series of phone calls, the first to his bank, then the airport and Switzerland. The last one was to Mr. Sommers. Then he made sure all the doors and windows were locked and with a light supper he went to bed.

The morning brought the sunshine and a new day. With just coffee for breakfast, he left the house and drove to the Sommers' cottage. He parked the Bentley next to the Ferrari.

Almost as soon as he arrived the front door of the cottage opened and Francesca came out to greet him.

'A new car?' she said as she approached him.

'Yes, I needed some transport to get back home.'

He put his arm around her shoulders and together they entered the cottage. Mr. Sommers was sitting in an arm chair.

'Have you any news, my boy?' he asked.

'Nothing concerning Louis La Ronde, but I do have a plan for your safety,' he answered.

Francesca excused herself to make coffee and Raymond started to explain. 'We must get you and Francesca out of the country. I have arranged with my cousin for you to stay with him for a few weeks. In that time, I will put a stop to La Ronde and his henchmen.'

'Out of the country,' repeated the old man, 'where are you going to send us?' he asked.

'To Switzerland,' replied Raymond, 'I've booked your flight; you leave this morning. My cousin Richard will meet you at the airport, he'll look after both of you until I contact you to say it's safe to return.'

Then Francesca returned carrying a tray of coffee, her father explained what Raymond had arranged for them.

'When is the flight?' she asked.

'Before midday, you should pack some things. We'll be leaving as soon as we can.'

Francesca offered no argument to stay; in her

mind she was relieved that her father would be safe and in less than an hour they were in Raymond's new Bentley and on their way to the airport.

'This is a very nice car, my boy,' remarked Mr. Sommers.

'I always thought I would like a Bentley,' Raymond smiled, 'when I found myself without any transport yesterday, I bought it to drive home.'

'What about the Ferrari?' asked Mr. Sommers as he took the keys for the Ferrari from his pocket and gave them to Raymond.

'I'll arrange to have it collected,' he replied.

When they arrived at the airport, they checked in and Raymond accompanied his friends to the departures lounge and stayed with them until their flight was called. He was glad that they would be safe, Mr. Sommers shook his hand.

'Thank you. You've done so much, how can I ever repay you?'

'We will have a party when you both come home,' he answered. Francesca put her arms around him and whispered, 'Thank you, Ray.'

Raymond watched through the panoramic windows as Mr. Sommers and his daughter boarded the aircraft. He waited until it was airborne and then he walked through the crowded airport back to his Bentley. As he drove out of the airport, he thought about Francesca and her father and was sure that Switzerland was the best place for them, at least for the moment.

But now he had to decide what action to take, 'I definitely don't want to fight La Ronde on his own ground,' he said aloud, 'and I don't want to involve the police.'

He had left the motorway and was travelling smoothly across Exmoor; he was still considering how he could stop La Ronde and his henchmen when he noticed a white Alfa Romeo in his mirrors, gaining on him rapidly.

'One problem at a time,' he said as he watched the sports car getting ever closer.

6

Joanna Sommers lived alone in one of the small cottages on Exmoor. She was full of life and always busy doing something. She was of medium build with blonde hair; she liked to call it yellow. Her blue eyes sparkled when she was happy, which was most of the time. She felt an affinity with the Native Americans and liked to dress in some of their traditional styles. Today she wore jeans with an Indian beaded belt and a buckskin jacket with fringes on both sleeves, the moccasins on her feet were decorated with Indian beadwork.

She was a gemmologist and made a living working with crystals, gems, precious and semiprecious stones. In her vast collection of crystals was a Herkimer diamond quartz crystal. It was faceted at both ends, a crystal made by nature. She had set it in a silver mount and suspended it on a very fine silver chain, which she wore almost all the time.

The cottage had a basement, which was unusual for the cottages on Exmoor. Joanna had made hers into a lapidary workshop and she had a great interest in Reiki.

The cottage belonged to her Uncle Rubin who lived in York and every time she visited him, he would tell her stories about Dick Turpin, the highwayman. The white Alfa Romeo that she drove had been a birthday present from him.

Joanna was happy with her life and this morning was like any other. The sun was shining, the sky was blue and all seemed right with the world until a black

45

Mercedes arrived outside and two men came to her door. When she opened it, they barged their way into the cottage.

'You're coming with us,' the bald-headed man said.

'Why? Who are you?'

'Because we've been told to bring you in,' he said, 'you know about gems and crystals and the Boss wants to talk to you.'

'Who's the Boss?'

'You'll find out all in good time,' was the answer. As she moved away from the men, she surreptitiously picked up the keys of the sports car without them noticing. The well-built man with the baldhead grabbed her.

'Come on Missy, it's time to go.'

Joanna kicked him in the shin. He promptly let her go and began hopping on one leg. She ran for the open door, closely followed by the other man. She let him get as far as the door frame and then slammed the door in his face. She heard him shout, 'Oh my nose! My nose, she broke my nose!'

Joanna ran for her car. Luckily it was an open sports car and she jumped over the door and started the engine as she landed in the driver's seat. She left to the sound of squealing tyres. The two men pushed their way out of the little cottage, the bald one limping and the other holding his nose. They started the Mercedes and left in hot pursuit. Joanna was now racing across Exmoor. Ahead of her she could see a Bentley. She was gaining on it rapidly and so she decided to overtake it.

Raymond watched the approaching car in his mirrors. It closed up the gap to his Bentley and passed him on what Raymond would have considered a blind bend. But now there was a black Mercedes saloon approaching from behind and, it too, passed the Bentley. Fortunately, there was no on-coming traffic.

Just out of curiosity, or maybe it was his sense of adventure, he pushed the accelerator to the floor. The Bentley smoothly changed down a gear and Raymond felt the acceleration push him back in his seat. He watched the speed increase and the RPM almost touch the red zone before it automatically changed gear. He steered the car around a left bend keeping it close to the bushes and then allowing it to slide smoothly towards the centre of the road. It was instinct to push the pedal to the floor again, but now he could see the two cars ahead of him, and they had stopped. He allowed the Bentley to slow down.

As he approached, he observed two men trying to push a girl into the back seat of the black Marauder. Stopping the Bentley behind the other two cars he leaped out and grabbed one of the men, spinning him around to face him, he landed an uppercut to his chin. This sent him stumbling backwards.

'Oh! I've bitten my tongue!' he exclaimed. Raymond grabbed the other man by his shoulders and pulled him backwards out of the car tripping him as he did. He rose to his feet and said, 'Spade!' Raymond noticed a blood-soaked bandage around his left wrist.

'You great bald Ox!' shouted the girl.

The two men stood together, one with blood flowing from his mouth. Raymond pulled the girl away from the Mercedes and placed himself between her and the assailants.

'Why do you want her?'

'This is not going to go well for you, Spade,' said

47

the bald-headed man, 'you are interfering, again!'

They began to advance; this time Raymond took up a karate stance and called to them by name. 'Oliver, Victor, do you really want to risk your lives?' he waited for a reaction.

The two men decided that retreat was the best form of defence, for they had both felt the effects of Raymond's fighting skills before. He stood clear of the Mercedes and they left, leaving tyre marks on the road as they did.

Raymond walked around the Alfa Romeo. There was a black mark on the driver's side front wing close to the head light.

'They made contact to stop you.'

'Yes,' she answered, 'and I haven't had it long. It was a birthday present from my uncle. The pigs, why me? I haven't done anything to upset anyone, at least not recently.'

Raymond liked her already, she was young and beautiful her blue eyes sparkled in the sunshine. Her golden hair flowed over her shoulders and she gave the impression of being seemingly carefree. There was something else, a feeling, but he couldn't put his finger on it just yet.

'My name is Raymond Spade,' he said offering her his hand. She took it.

'Joanna Sommers.'

'May I ask you Miss Sommers...?'

'Jo, call me Jo,' she said.

'Alright, Jo, May I ask you what that was all about?'

'They pushed their way into my cottage this morning and said their boss wanted to see me. They were about to get nasty and so I made a run for it. But,' she paused, 'how do they know you, Mr. Spade?'

'Please, call me Ray,' he said, 'They think that some friends of mine have some information that they want. I've just sent my friends to Switzerland while I try to stop those men and their boss. If they are showing an interest in you, may I suggest that you come back to my house, just until we know you're safe?'

Joanna agreed and slid into the driver's seat of her car. She started the engine. 'I'll follow you,' she said with a smile, her eyes sparkling again.

Raymond drove at a steady speed and the Alfa Romeo had no problem at all following him. The Bentley turned into a driveway; the Alfa Romeo followed and eventually stopped next to it.

Joanna stepped out of her car, looking intently up at the house, 'Is this all yours?'

'Yes,' Raymond answered. Come in, I'll show you around.'

'I've wanted to see inside this place for a long time; I've passed it many times on my way to see my father and sister. I always wondered what it was like inside.'

Raymond pushed open the large oak front door and they walked through the long oak panelled hallway and upstairs. After wandering around the house, they eventually arrived in Raymond's favourite room, the lounge on the second floor that looked out over the grounds.

The walls were wood panelled and the fireplace was laid with logs for burning. On the mantelpiece lay the gun that Raymond had taken from Oliver, the bald-headed man. Directly opposite, hanging on the wall was a woven tapestry of a wild deer.

'Oh Ray, it's beautiful!' she exclaimed.

'Jo, I wonder if I can ask you a favour...' She interrupted him.

'What do you need?'

'Would you take me to collect my other car?'

'Certainly, where is it? And what is it?'

'It's not far from here; and you can try and guess on the way.'

Raymond picked up the keys for the Ferrari and they left the house. It wasn't long before they were winding their way through the country roads. Joanna continued guessing as she drove.

'It's a Rolls Royce?'

'No.'

'It's a Land Rover?'

'No.'

'It's a Mini?'

'No.'

'Oh, I give up. What is it?'

'You need to see it to appreciate it.'

'Is it a British car?' she asked.

'No.'

'Which country does it come from?'

'The same country as yours,' he answered.

'What, a Maserati?'

'No.'

'Oh, come on, Ray, a Fiat?'

'No.'

But now they were getting close to Mr. Sommers' cottage.

'Slow down, Jo, we need the next driveway.'

'The next driveway,' she repeated, 'this is my father's house.'

Joanna glanced quickly at Raymond then slowed

down and entered the driveway, she brought the car to a stop. 'You know my father and sister, Francesca?'

'Yes, I do, I have just come from the airport, I have sent them to Switzerland to keep them safe, and away from those two men you met this morning. My cousin Richard will look after them until it is safe for them to return.'

Joanna parked next to the car that was there, then she recognised it for what it was.

'Oh my God, it's a Ferrari,' she said, 'I would have never guessed, you looked so slow in your Bentley.'

Raymond unlocked the Ferrari and slide into the driver's seat. He turned the key and the red car burst onto life. Joanna bent down next to the driver's window.

'What a sound!' she said admiringly.

'Do you know your way back to The Five Pines?' he asked.

'Yes,' she answered.

'I'll see you there.'

She watched as Raymond reversed the Ferrari out of the driveway and then she did the same with the Alfa Romeo. By the time she was ready to move the Ferrari had gone. She pressed the pedal to the floor and, although she couldn't see the Ferrari, she considered herself in pursuit.

When Raymond reached his driveway, he waited until he could see the white Alfa Romeo, then he entered. The two cars were driven slowly through the grounds to the turning circle and there they were parked next to the Bentley. The Ferrari and the Alfa Romeo looked very impressive next to each other.

'I like your taste in cars,' Joanna said as they entered the house.

The hours that followed were used to prepare a bedroom for Joanna. Though she had only known Raymond for a short time she knew he was a good man, all her Reiki senses told her so.

Raymond lit the log fire and prepared an evening meal that they both enjoyed. Then Raymond produced two very large glasses of brandy and they sat on the big settee watching the flickering flames.

'I met you father and sister in Austria. A man named Louis La Ronde kidnapped your father because he thought he could tell him how to bypass the alarm systems that he was lecturing about. Your father told him that code numbers wouldn't switch the alarms off, and he didn't know any combinations as they could be changed easily every twenty-four hours if necessary. La Ronde wants to steal a diamond, and he wants me to help him. But why they wanted to kidnap you, I have no idea.'

'I am a gemmologist, that is, I know about precious stones.'

Joanna looked around the room and changing the subject said, 'It's a big house, isn't it? Do you ever get lonely?'

'I try not to,' he answered. Then her eyes alighted on the gun on the shelf above the fireplace. She rose from the settee and picked it up.

'What is this for?' she asked.

'I took it from Oliver, you know, the bald-headed man.'

'You didn't take it today,' she stated.

'No, not today. It was a few days ago.' He moved closer to her and took the gun as he knew it was loaded, and replaced it on the mantelpiece.

'Jo,' he said, 'I'm concerned for your safety.' Just

then they heard a rap at the front door.

'That's odd, nobody ever calls on me,' he picked up the Smith & Wesson and went to investigate. He was only away for a few minutes and when he returned Louis La Ronde entered the room ahead of Raymond, his hands in the air. His trench coat hanging loosely around him revealing the jewel encrusted flintlock pistol in its holster.

'Please, sit down.' Raymond gestured with the gun in his hand, 'I knew that if I stayed here long enough, you or your men would show up sooner or later. If it's a fight you are looking for, I would rather fight on my terms and on my ground. What do you want?' he asked abruptly.

'I hear you met my two men again earlier today. They are looking forward to getting their hands on you. But enough of that.' He turned his attention to Joanna.

'Miss Sommers, it would seem that you know who I am.'

'I have never met you before.'

'But I know about you, I know that you are a gemmologist and I know you know that the Snowflake Diamond will soon be displayed in London,' he paused, 'I want you to make a copy for me. I know you can, I've heard about your expertise, so this is what I propose. You make me a copy in two weeks and I won't cause your Uncle Rubin any harm.'

La Ronde stood up and totally ignored the gun that Raymond was holding, he started to wander around the room.

'You have some nice stuff here; the cars looked very impressive too, I can see why money was no incentive for you to work for me, and you still have

Oliver's gun, I'll leave it with you. He wants to claim it himself.' He looked at Joanna. 'You have two weeks from now. Take it to your Uncle Rubin's house. I will be there, waiting for you.'

He walked to the door of the lounge and placed his hand on the exposed flintlock pistol under his trench coat. 'I'll see myself out.'

Raymond and Joanna watched from the bay windows as Louis La Ronde drove a black Mercedes the length of the driveway and left the grounds.

'Can you do what he asks?' enquired Raymond as he replaced the Smith & Wesson back on the shelf above the fireplace.

'Now we know his interest in me. I am a gemmologist,' she said, 'I think I can create something, but it won't be like the real thing.'

'Tomorrow we'll have to go back to your cottage; you can show me what you have. If you don't have the gems that you need to make a copy I'll obtain some.'

Joanna agreed and the evening passed quietly after Louis La Ronde's departure. They sipped their brandy and talked about gemstones and many other things. Around eleven o'clock they went to their separate rooms.

They were both up early the next morning and after a quick breakfast they took the Ferrari to Joanna's cottage. Joanna was going to show Raymond her lapidary workshop. When they arrived Joanna had a momentary shock: the front door was open. Then she realised that was the way she had left it when she was chased out by Oliver and Victor yesterday. It felt like a long time ago.

They left the Ferrari on the road outside the cottage and went inside. She rolled back part of the carpet to reveal a trap door. Opening it they descended down a wooden flight of stairs into the basement.

Joanna switched the lights on and Raymond was amazed as he looked around. This was a fully equipped gemmologist's lapidary workshop. There were work benches, clamps, drills, polishers and even a laser drill and cutter. Around the walls were diagrams of cutting procedures, all the different cuts that were possible depending on the hardness of the gemstone. Then Raymond noticed, hanging in a corner, a pendant made of beads and colourful threads, sown together in the most beautiful spider-web designs. He reached out and touched it.

'What is it?'

'It's a dream catcher, the American Indians make them traditionally,' she answered.

'It's breath-taking, Jo. I don't just mean the dream catcher, I mean all of this.'

'It's all I need, it's my life's work,' she said. Then she opened a drawer and produced a poster-sized piece of paper. She spread it out on one of the benches.

'What am I looking at?'

'This is the Snowflake Diamond. A photograph doesn't do it justice, see these tiny sparkles in it? They are created by fissures, tiny flaws in the gem; they reflect the light in so many different directions inside it, no other gem has such fire. When you rotate it, they move, it's a miracle of nature. See how the centre looks like a snowflake that has been magnified. I could cut another stone into the same shape, but it would be virtually impossible to create a sparkle like that inside another gem. Isn't it ironic that its flaws are what makes it so stunning, so unique? It's one of the reasons I love working with diamonds.'

She thought for a moment, and then began to deal with the problem in hand.

'I can make a copy but not out of a real diamond, it would have to be rock crystal or quartz crystal, but it wouldn't sparkle like the real one.'

'We just need something to give to La Ronde, as long as it's the right shape, that's all he wants.'

'So, this is why I was chased out of my house yesterday by those two men.'

'Whether it was Oliver or Victor, or as it turned out Louis La Ronde himself the result would have been the same. We need a copy of the diamond to give to La Ronde if we are going to keep your Uncle Rubin safe,' stated Raymond.

'My uncle is a good man. He was injured in an accident while serving with the armed forces and since he's turned seventy, he doesn't go out much now.' She looked around, 'this cottage belongs to him. He knew I wanted to be a gemmologist and so he had a basement dug out for me and all the equipment installed. He only asks that I visit him occasionally. He gave me the Alfa Romeo for my birthday.'

'I'll make sure that La Ronde doesn't harm him,' Raymond said reassuringly.

'Thank you!' she said, her blue eyes sparkling. She felt safe with Raymond, and she needed to believe that everything would work out right.

'I better get started on making a copy of the Snowflake Diamond.'

'I'll stay with you until you have,' volunteered Raymond.

Joanna spent the whole day examining all the

crystals that she had in stock and by the next afternoon she had chosen the crystal that she was going to work with.

'This is it,' she called to Raymond. He came down the wooden stairs into the basement. She was holding a crystal close to a light on one of the work benches.

'Isn't it beautiful?' she said, 'These crystals are used in Reiki. It is a Herkimer Diamond Quartz found in the Mohawk River. The first ones were found in about 1725. A double terminated crystal; a crystal with two naturally faceted ends. I'd forgotten I had this one until I found it in one of the drawers with some other crystals. I wear a similar one as a pendent; it can detect things, you know.' She showed Raymond the one around her neck, a small crystal hanging on a simple silver chain. 'It can detect bad vibration, it vibrates when someone lies to you and it can warn you when you are in the presence of a spirit or ghost.' She turned her attention back to the one she was holding, 'I'll cut this one because I need a flat surface to cut facets into it. The lower half of the crystal should be alright as it is.'

'Is there anything I can do to help?' asked Raymond.

'I think we should have something to eat, I'm starving,' Joanna grinned.

'That's not surprising, you've been down here, living on coffee and the occasional sandwich for the last two days,' Raymond told her. So, it was decided that they would go out for dinner; now she had found the right crystal, work could wait until tomorrow morning.

It was a welcome break from the workshop. The food was very good and the wine was intoxicating. The days passed in this manner, Joanna would work all hours in the basement and Raymond would make her take a break occasionally. So it went on, the days running into each other, until one day about lunch time Joanna emerged from the basement, looking for Raymond. When she found him, she was holding something in her hand.

'Look at this!' she said excitedly. Raymond looked at it. Now he knew why she was a gemmologist.

'It's magnificent,' he said taking the crystal from her and turning it over in his hand. It was so exquisite, he couldn't believe it wasn't the real thing.

'How much time do we have before we have to deliver it?' she asked.

'We must be with your uncle in two days.'

Joanna went back to the basement and collected a soft chamois leather bag. When she returned she took the crystal from Raymond and carefully placed it inside. They were ready to leave, so they made sure that the cottage was locked securely and then they left to return to Raymond's house,, The Five Pines.

The journey was uneventful and for that they were thankful. Raymond spent the next day getting the Bentley ready for its trip to York. Other than that, they tried to relax with a good meal, wine and a large brandy. The following day they started their journey about mid-morning.

Raymond was dressed in casual clothes, corduroy jacket and trousers, and Joanna had resorted to her buckskin jacket with the frills on the sleeves, and jeans; on her feet she still wore moccasins. She carried the soft leather bag with the crystal inside it.

They drove in silence for a while, giving Joanna

time to think, then she said, 'I don't want to give this to La Ronde.'

'If it will take La Ronde's interest away from your uncle, it'll be worth it.'

'La Ronde is not worthy of possessing a Herkimer Quartz Crystal. Do you know that it will vibrate if the person you are talking to is dishonest?'

'He is that,' said Raymond.

'With its high vibrational frequency, it may even assist in telepathic communication. It can recall dreams and help make them vivid.'

'That is a lot from one crystal,' remarked Raymond.

'It is. I don't think he should have it. This crystal can help in spiritualism, healing, meditation and magic. It could also summon a guardian angel. He could do a lot of damage with it if he knows how to use it,' she said with concern.

The journey passed quickly as they discussed the Herkimer Quartz Crystal and the rights and wrongs of giving it to Louis La Ronde. As they entered the driveway, Raymond was surprised to see that the house and grounds were almost as big as The Five Pines. Joanna was still explaining about the Herkimer Quartz Crystal.

'They are natural objects of perfection,' she was saying, 'Oh,' she said with surprise, 'we've arrived.'

'Yes, we have, now let's see if we can give La Ronde the crystal and take your uncle somewhere safe.'

They left the car and walked slowly to the front door. It was quite dark when Joanna tapped the door knocker, they waited for some kind of response.

'My Herkimer crystal is vibrating, Ray, this is not good.' Raymond touched the crystal that was around Joanna's neck, and, yes, it was vibrating. Then the door opened and Louis La Ronde greeted them.

'Mr. Spade and Miss Sommers, good evening. Do you have something for me?' Joanna handed him the leather bag. He took it and looked inside, putting his hand in he removed the crystal and looked at it.

'Very good, Miss Sommers,' he replaced it into the soft leather bag. 'I shall be leaving you, but you are welcome to see your uncle. He is inside waiting for you.'

Louis Ra Ronde walked away along the driveway and was lost from their sight.

'Come on, Jo; let's make sure that your uncle is unhurt.' Raymond pushed the front door to open it a little more and, though it was dark, they entered cautiously. Joanna tried flicking a switch but no lights came on. There was a candelabra and a box of matches on a small table in the hallway, Raymond could hardly see them, but he took a match from the box and lit the candles one by one. Joanna closed the front door behind them.

'Uncle Rubin!' she called, peering around the shadowy hallway. There was no reply.

'He should be here, Uncle Rubin! It's me... Jo,' there was still no reply. Raymond was just about to say something to reassure her when he saw something move on the staircase. A man sprang down the stairs and landed in front of them, then vanished into the dark shadows in the candlelit hallway. Joanna gave a little scream of fright and jumped back away from him. Raymond stepped in front of her and stood his ground, peering into the shadows. Then the man moved slowly into the candlelight.

7

He was dressed in a Harlequin costume with a crimson mask hiding his face; in his hand was a very large Bowie knife, the steel blade glinted in the candle light. He tossed it casually from one hand to the other. Raymond stepped back. Taking Joanna with him, he pushed her to safety behind him. Harlequin advanced slowly and attacked. The blade flashed very close to Raymond's face. He moved back again taking Joanna with him.

Harlequin took up the gap between himself and Raymond, still playing with the knife, as he tossed it from one hand to the other. Raymond saw his chance and stepped forward quickly. The heel of his right palm smashed into the Harlequin's forehead just above his nose. He dropped the Bowie knife and staggered backwards, blinded by his watering eyes.

'In here!' said Raymond as he opened a door in the dimly lit hallway. They rushed inside and he slammed the door shut. They stood poised, facing the door, waiting for the Harlequin to enter. A few moments passed in silence then Joanna asked, 'Where is he? Why isn't he following us?'

The room they found themselves in was dark and empty, except for a large pedestal with a glass dome on top that housed a flashing blue light. Raymond knew this was not good.

'Obviously whoever he was wanted us in here.' Then another voice was heard, 'Correct, and there is no escape,' it said. The light began flashing in a steady rhythm; blue fluorescent pulsating light filled the room. Just under the glass dome was a speaker, the source of the voice.

'Don't look at the light,' Raymond said with some urgency, 'it will have a hypnotic effect on us. We must get out of here,' he added as he examined the door. There was no door handle, the whole wooden surface of the door was completely smooth. The situation seemed hopeless.

'What can we do, Ray?'

'Stay calm and try not to look at the light,' he answered softly. They tried to look away from the light and shaded their eyes with their hands but even when they closed their eyes, the insistent blue pulse was visible. They began to feel drowsy as the room around them slowly disappeared and was replaced by a graveyard. It was twilight and numerous headstones protruded through the leaf-covered ground. There was no sound, no breeze. The leaves made no noise as they were disturbed when they walked slowly between the headstones.

'What is this place?' asked Joanna.

'I don't know,' Raymond answered, 'no birds, no wind, no moonlight, just that blue pulsing light. Jo, I don't think any of this is real.'

Then they heard a voice, 'It's an unfriendly place to die.'

Raymond had heard that phrase before; they turned around to be confronted by the Harlequin, still holding the knife. Raymond recognised him, even though the semi-hypnotic state that he was in, 'Victor the Vampire,' he said.

The Harlequin attacked without warning, lunging and slashing. He went for Joanna first and she cried out as the blade cut deep into her face and arms as she tried to protect herself. Raymond moved to try to help her, but he was slow. The Harlequin spun around and found his mark, sinking the weapon into Raymond's stomach.

Joanna screamed wildly, her face and arms covered in blood, she watched helplessly as Raymond dropped to his knees, his eyes glazed over and his face twisted in pain. The Harlequin pulled the blade from Raymond's body and Joanna just kept on screaming as she watched Raymond dying at her feet.

Then Harlequin said loudly, 'Every time you think of the Snowflake Diamond or hear the name Louis La Ronde, this is what you will see!'

He backed away into the shadowy graveyard and was lost from sight. She sank to her knees next to Raymond, her hands covering her face; Raymond slowly began to move and pulled himself to his knees and knelt beside her.

'Jo, Jo, it's alright, it's all over.' A comforting hand touched her and he helped her to her feet. They were back in the room with the blue pulsating light, and unharmed. Joanna, trying to collect her senses, turned to Raymond, bewildered, and asked, 'What happened to us?'

'I think we have been put into a hypnotic state and we have seen what was suggested to us, but we must get out of this place.' Joanna was still shaken from her experience.

'Ray, I saw you die!' Still the dome continued to fill the room with flashes of blue light. Raymond took the small knife from his pocket and stuck the razor-sharp blade into the smooth wood of the door. He pulled gently on the knife and the door began to open, but then he started to feel drowsy again. He looked around him; the room had disappeared, he was back in the graveyard again. Not far away was a small group of people standing around an open grave. He walked slowly towards them. There were two men dressed in black and Joanna was with them. A coffin lay beside them. Raymond was closer now and he could see the inscription on the tombstone, it read, 'Raymond Spade. Rest in Peace'.

'Miss Sommers, what does it mean to you if I were to say, Snowflake Diamond?'

Joanna shouted, 'No!' she didn't want to see that hypnotic hallucination play out again and took a step back from the open grave. She remembered that Raymond had said this is a hypnotic suggestion. She tried to clear her mind and said, 'I'm a gemmologist, I know about crystals!'

'That's the wrong answer, Miss Sommers.'

The men lifted the lid off the coffin and one of them took off his black coat to reveal his Harlequin costume beneath, he also took the Bowie knife from his belt and pointed it at Joanna.

'Get into your coffin, Spade, or she won't live to witness your burial.' Raymond could do nothing; he was too far away to try to disarm the Harlequin. So he walked over to the coffin, hoping that Joanna might do something to give him a chance.

'Lie down, Spade.' Raymond did as he was asked and lay in the coffin. The twilight of the graveyard was lost as the coffin lid was screwed into place. He felt the coffin move as it was lowered into the hole in the earth. Fear was a feeling he knew well; it is a fool who does not fear a battle, but fear was a feeling he had learned to control. He had felt it many times while driving the prototype vehicles on the track. When the

65

instruction was given: increase the speed until something fails. This was the feeling he felt now as he lay entombed, listening to the shovelfuls of earth landing on the coffin lid.

'You can have the coffin exhumed if you never speak of Louis La Ronde or the Snowflake Diamond again,' the Harlequin said as he pointed the Bowie knife close to Joanna's throat. Joanna could only see half of his face as his crimson mask was covering the rest. The two men looked at her, the one with the shovel stopped throwing earth onto the coffin. She carefully moved around the blade of the Bowie knife and closer to the edge of the grave, the coffin was barely visible now and the blue pulsing light continued to flash. The Harlequin grabbed her arm.

'That's close enough!' he said. He put his arms around her and she began to struggle with him as she tried to stop the blade of the Bowie knife from cutting her throat.

In the darkness, Raymond placed his palms against the wooden lid and pushed slowly. With his back against the floor and his hands against the lid he pushed, just like all the press ups he had ever done. He pushed and pushed, then a focus came over him, as if trapped in a burning car (which he had been on more than one occasion) the strength that comes from within, in a life or death situation increased. Adrenaline raced through his veins. He pushed with all his might and then something gave way. The screws that were holding the coffin lid in place ripped their threads out of the wood and the lid flew into the air with a mighty force.

Raymond leapt out, ready for confrontation. The coffin wasn't in a hole, and the screws holding the coffin lid were no more than small self-tappers. The coffin was lying on the floor of the room, the blue light still flashing silently. The Harlequin was holding Joanna, and the other man with the spade was going through the motions of shovelling earth, making the hypnotic illusion more convincing.

'Hello, Oliver,' Raymond said as he wrestled the shovel from him and tossed it onto the floor. Raymond swiftly put a sleeper hold on his opponent, for that is how Raymond thought of him, and squeezed until the man became unconscious. Then he let him fall to the ground.

Although the blue light continued to flash, its hypnotic effect was no longer affecting Raymond. He could see clearly what the two men had been trying to do and, although it was working on Joanna, he knew how to focus his mind. He had done so, many times when he was working as a test driver.

'Enough!' he shouted, and then he went for the Harlequin, pushing Joanna away from him and tearing the crimson mask from his face in one movement.

'Victor. What a surprise,' he said sarcastically.

He grabbed the man by the throat with one hand and took the Bowie knife away from him with the other. He tightened his grip and started to choke the life out of him. Then his aggression subsided and his actions became less fierce.

'Who is La Ronde's client?' he asked.

He released his grip on Victor's throat so that he could suck some air in.

'I've had enough of playing games; it's your choice, tell me or die.' This sounded final to Victor and so he answered with a croak in his voice, 'Captain Journal, Captain James Journal, he wants the

Snowflake Diamond. He's La Ronde's client.'

'When you have the diamond, how is it to be collected?'

'Captain Journal doesn't collect, we must deliver it.'

'Where and when?'

'I can't tell you that, it is more than my life is worth.' Raymond tightened his grip on Victor's throat. He began to tap Raymond's arm as wrestlers do when a submission is won. Raymond allowed Victor to take in some air.

'Forty-eight hours from the time it is obtained, to Tresco, one of the Isles of Scilly.'

'You mean from when it's stolen,' said Raymond as he pushed Victor away from him. 'Go. Don't cross me again.' As he said this, he flipped the Bowie knife into the air and caught it by the blade bringing the carved bone handle down on the flashing blue dome with such force that it shattered the blue glass to reveal a flashing strobe light.

Oliver was just coming around and started to get up, Victor helped him to his feet. Raymond went to the door and sank the blade of the Bowie knife into it; then he opened the door easily by pulling on the handle of the knife.

Victor walked to the door, Oliver leaning heavily on his partner in crime.

'Our orders were to frighten you. We could have just shot you, but the boss is still hoping you will join him. I know the hypnosis hasn't worked on you, but it might have an effect on Miss Sommers. You know, post-hypnotic suggestion.'

'Why are you doing this?' asked Raymond.

'Money. La Ronde pays well.' Victor and Oliver

left the room. Raymond helped Joanna to her feet and made sure she was unhurt. He pulled the Bowie knife out of the door and, taking it with him, they also left the room.

They emerged into the hallway, the candles still burning on the small table. The front door had been left open and there was no sign of Oliver and Victor. They both paused, just waiting for something else to happen, but all was quiet.

'What was all that about!?' Joanna asked.

'I think they were trying to erase our memories of giving the Snowflake Diamond that you made to Louis La Ronde, and then replacing them with the made-up horror of the grave yard using hypnosis.' Then he said something that Joanna wasn't expecting, 'Oliver and Victor were not trying to kill us. This was an exercise in fright. They would have killed us when I first met them in Austria, but something has changed. This charade with the flashing blue light could have worked, but there are better, more permanent ways to dispose of us. Louis La Ronde still wants me to work for him.' Then he changed the subject and said, 'Let's see if we can find your uncle.'

After looking in all the rooms downstairs they tried the next floor, then Raymond asked, 'Does this house have an attic?'

'Yes, do you think they locked him in up there?'

'It's a good place to keep him out of the way,' he replied.

Raymond led the way, climbing the stairs two at a time. He arrived at the locked attic door first and Joanna followed, 'Uncle Rubin!' she called, 'Are you in there?'

'Yes, my dear,' said a voice from the other side of

the door, 'I'm locked in.' Raymond looked around but there was no key to be seen.

'Stand back from the door,' he instructed and then he delivered a kick to the lock and the door was flung open with great force, pieces of wood and a few screws landing on the floor. Joanna entered and hugged her uncle.

'I was so afraid that they may have hurt you!' she said.

'It is good to see you, my dear, I was worried what they'd do to you,' he said. Rubin was an older man, Raymond estimated, in his early seventies. His hair was grey and thinning on top and he was wearing a dark blue velvet smoking jacket and a dark green pair of corduroy trousers.

Raymond led the way down the stairs and Joanna and Rubin followed him. When they reached the hallway, Raymond said, 'I think it would be best if you came and stayed with us for a few days.'

'Is that necessary? Do you think they'll come back?'

'I'm not sure, but I wouldn't like to take the risk.'

'I thank you, but only if I'm not intruding.'

'You're not intruding,' Joanna said with a smile.

'Then I just need to collect a few things first.'

Rubin wandered around the rooms on the ground floor and in a few minutes he returned. He was putting a handful of his best Havanas into the inside pocket of his smoking jacket and as he passed his black cloak and walking stick, he picked them up and said, 'I am ready to go.'

Joanna blew out the candles on the small table and Rubin locked the front door. They all left the house together and as they walked across the driveway Rubin remarked, 'Yours?' pointing at the Bentley.

'Yes,' replied Raymond.

'You wait until you see his other car,' Joanna said with a smile.

The journey to The Five Pines was comfortable in the Bentley. Rubin asked a lot of questions about the men in his house and was quite indignant when he explained about being locked in the attic.

'I would have given them a good fight in my younger days,' he said. After about an hour he fell asleep in the back seat and Raymond and Joanna decided during the course of their conversation that both she and her uncle should stay with Raymond, at least for the moment.

It was very late when the Bentley stopped next to the Ferrari and the Alfa Romeo. They woke Rubin who, perhaps because it was dark or because he was not fully awake, didn't notice the other cars on the driveway. Raymond unlocked the large oak door and invited his new friends inside.

8

They went into the house and Joanna prepared one of the bedrooms for her uncle. Raymond placed the Bowie knife on the shelf above the fireplace next to the Smith & Wesson and then made some coffee. At last they were all in the lounge, sitting on the large settee.

'It is very good of you to invite me to stay; I must confess that I was a little nervous of the thought of being alone in my house, those men found entry so easily. Do you think that they may come back?'

Raymond tried to explain, 'Their only interest in you was to threaten Jo. You see, they are going to steal a world-famous diamond, and they wanted Jo to make a copy of it. She did and we gave it to their boss when we arrived at your house. Now, with any luck, this shouldn't involve you anymore.'

Joanna was safe but she still felt uneasy, she frowned and then asked, 'Ray, what happened to us? Was any of that real? It was all so frightening.'

'Hypnosis,' he answered. 'It was all in our minds. It's like an incident I heard about some time ago involving a helicopter. It crashed because the pilot was watching another helicopter that was flying in formation just below him. It had a blue light showing on its fuselage and the rotor blades gave the impression of a flashing blue light, a strobe effect that fixated the pilot. That's what happened to us.'

'What happened to the pilot?'

'The aircraft crashed but he was unhurt. I just used the helicopter as an example of the use of a blue flashing light to induce a hypnotic state.'

'But why would they go to such effort?'

'Evidently they wanted to make sure that we forgot about Louis La Ronde and the crystal that you made for him.'

'It all seemed very real to me,' stated Joanna.

'For an example, they had a real coffin and Oliver had a real spade. He went through the motions and your mind filled in the rest. As for the Bowien knife, Victor waved it around, shouting his threats. The knife was real enough, he touched you with the dull edge of the blade, and you made the rest happen in your mind.'

'What about you, did you believe it too?' she asked.

'Yes, I have to admit it was very frightening,' agreed Raymond, 'and that was my weakness, but once I was able to focus on something real like the coffin I was told to get into, I was able to disconnect myself from the situation. I know how to be very single minded, like driving a car at speed well beyond its safety limits, your whole being comes alive, and your concentration is at its peak. But,' he added, 'when the lid of the coffin was fastened down, I couldn't see the blue light, I realised what was happening and forced the coffin lid open. It was only fastened by a few self-tapping screws and I was able to open it easily. They didn't have to stage much as the whole thing was conducted in darkness with the exception of the flashing blue light.'

'Do you think they have left something in my mind?' Joanna asked.

'I don't know Jo. Victor did say something about post hypnotic suggestion, but I think he was just trying to give me something else to worry about.'

Then Rubin joined the conversation, 'I still feel safe here with both of you, they were very unpleasant men,' he shuddered. They continued talking late into the night but eventually retired. Raymond was at a loss, not knowing what to call the old man so he said, 'Should I address you as Mr. Sommers? You're Jo's father's brother, aren't you?'

'Yes, I am, but if you don't mind, I would like you to call me Uncle Rubin, the same as Jo, it sounds so much more informal, don't you think?'

'Yes, I do,' there was a pause, 'Uncle Rubin, I think I should tell you that I know your brother and his other daughter, Francesca.'

'You know Michael and Francesca, isn't it a small world,' he smiled and dismissed the statement, then added. 'Goodnight my boy.'

'Goodnight, Uncle Rubin,' he replied.

Joanna and Rubin left Raymond alone and they went to bed. Before Raymond could rest for the night, he checked the whole house and made sure all the doors and windows were locked. Then he retired to his bedroom.

The activities of yesterday had taken a toll on Raymond and he slept longer than he would normally. When he did get up, Joanna had breakfast ready for him. He sat down at the breakfast table and it wasn't just the full cooked breakfast that caught his eye, there was an envelope propped against the marmalade. He picked it up and opened it while Joanna poured some coffee for him.

'My dear friend,

I am writing to thank you for sending us to Switzerland. Your cousin Richard has taken us in and we are living with him as though we were part of his family. He has taken some time off from his work to take us sight-seeing. It has been like a holiday. Richard says we can stay as long as we need to. I do feel we are taking advantage of him. When I told him about Louis La Ronde, he told me that you had made him aware of the danger. He hardly ever leaves us alone, he is watching us all the time like a guardian angel. He said if La Ronde could find us in Austria, he could follow us to Switzerland, which I did find a bit unnerving at first. He seems to be a lot like you and now both of us feel safe with him around.

Richard sends you his best wishes; he says that he hopes that you and he can meet one day soon.

That is all my news, I hope you are not having any more reprisals from Louis La Ronde, and that the problem will soon be resolved.

I am your friend,

M. Sommers.

Raymond finished his breakfast and showed the letter to Rubin and Joanna. They agreed that Francesca and her father were in safe hands. Then Raymond suggested a day out. 'I would like to take you to meet some friends of mine.'

He saw Joanna and Rubin into his Bentley and then made his way to the test track that had been his place of work for many years. It wasn't a long drive and it was about mid-morning when they arrived. He parked the Bentley where he usually parked his Ferrari and they walked to the office. Raymond opened the door and went in, but the office was deserted. 'They must be testing a car,' he said so he led his friends to the track.

They arrived just in time to see a new sports car

travelling at very high speed and then it suddenly tried to stop. The front wheels locked up and smoke poured off the tyres. Eventually it came to rest. A group of men ran from the side of the track and opened the driver's door. Raymond walked towards the car. As the driver climbed out, he saw Raymond and walked towards him.

'Ray! Are you looking for a job?' The man was big black and looked very strong. He grabbed Raymond by the shoulders, soon the other men joined them and enjoyment and joviality filed the air. Eventually the shouting and dancing stopped and Raymond was allowed to speak. 'Sam, I would like to introduce you to my two very good friends, Rubin Sommers and his niece, Joanna.'

'I am very pleased to meet you,' said Sam. He turned and said, 'These men are all friends of Ray's too, they are the safety team, we all worked together until Ray retired.' Sam looked at Raymond, 'We could do with a good test driver,' he added.

The afternoon passed quickly and the men all finished work early. Raymond invited Sam back to The Five Pines for an evening meal. Sam accepted the offer and travelled with his friends in the Bentley. He had been to Raymond's house before and, though not surprised, he did feel a little unsure of himself as he walked on the thick dark red piled carpet in his working shoes.

The meal didn't take long to prepare and Sam soon felt at home with his friends. After the meal, Raymond offered brandy and everyone accepted it. They talked about old times and filled Joanna in on any questions she had about Raymond's previous life. Rubin excused himself saying he was going to indulge in one of his Havana's and left the room.

Sam drank more than one brandy, in fact he drank so many that Raymond persuaded him to stay for the night. Rubin didn't return after his cigar, he just went to his room and his bed and, once Joanna had gone to her room, Raymond explained the situation regarding Louis La Ronde to Sam. It was very late when at last Raymond showed Sam to a room that was prepared for his friend. When he left Sam, he checked all the locks and windows before he retired for the night.

* * *

The following morning Rubin was the first to rise. He had prepared breakfast and was waiting for the rest of the household to join him. He had been listening to the radio and had heard a report about the theft of a diamond.

When the others had all arrived for breakfast, Rubin related what he had heard on the radio. 'I have just been listening to a news report,' he said, 'and I think La Ronde and his men have succeeded in stealing the diamond. It has not been revealed how. It had been transported to the British Museum in London and after it had been placed in its display case, one of the experts said he wanted a closer look at it, then it was found to be a copy.'

'Then it's a fair bet that it was the Snowflake Diamond,' stated Raymond, 'that leaves us forty-eight hours or less, to go to the Isles of Scilly and find Captain James Journal.' He paused, 'That doesn't give us much time. I better make some travel arrangements.'

'Who is James Journal, and how do you know

that the Snowflake Diamond will be taken to the Isles of Scilly?' asked Rubin.

'Victor the Vampire, the Harlequin, he told me. I am inclined to believe him considering I didn't give him much of a choice.'

Raymond rose from the table and as he was about to leave the room Joanna asked, 'Why must we intercept the Snowflake Diamond? Can't we just let them have it?'

'You made the copy and that could lead the police to you.'

'Ray is right,' said Rubin, 'the police will want some answers from you when they find out that you made the copy, they may even jump to the conclusion that you are working with La Ronde.'

'I hadn't thought of that.' Joanna looked worried,' Can I come with you?'

'It could be dangerous,' Raymond warned her.

'Please, Ray?'

'Very well, we leave tonight. If I remember correctly, the ship, the Scillonian, sails early every morning from Penzance, it carries the mail and passengers to the Island of Saint Mary's.'

'Will you be alright here?' she asked her Uncle Rubin.

'Yes of course, don't worry about me,' he said.

Sam had been listing to all this and he said, 'Giving up danger and excitement, that's what you told me. It sounds like your life is more dangerous and exciting now than when you were driving for me. Would you like me to come with you?'

'Not this time Sam, but if you can spare the time from your work schedule, I would appreciate it if you could stay with Rubin until we get back.'

'I can do that, there isn't much on at the test track for the next week.'

'You're both welcome to anything you may need while we are away.'

'Thank you, Ray,' said Rubin.

It didn't take long to pack a few things, then Raymond and Joanna left the house. Rubin and Sam watched from the bay window as the Bentley moved along the driveway through the grounds and vanished out onto the main road.

Rubin turned away from the windows, picked up his walking stick and sat down on the big settee. He twisted the top of the stick and pulled, to expose a long blade. He ran his fingers along the length of it, looked at it and after pausing for a moment, replaced it. 'If only you could talk,' he said.

'It can't, but I can,' said Sam, 'I haven't seen a sword stick as close as this before, it looks like it could be an antique.'

'It is, it's Victorian, it was made around 1888, about the time of Jack the Ripper. I have never had cause to use it, but with the current state of affairs with Louis La Ronde and his henchmen, I feel safer with it than without it.'

He was not alone in this big house because Sam was with him, but in his own house which was about the same size, he would be alone and vulnerable especially after being visited by La Ronde and his men. It was this that made him decide that he was not going home.

He leaned back on the settee and took one of his Havana's from his pocket, 'Would you like one, Sam,' he asked. Sam declined the offer, 'My life is dangerous

79

enough without smoking, though I have always liked the aroma.'

'I hope you don't mind if I do,' he struck a match and lit the cigar. Watching the smoke rising slowly into the air, he felt safe, especially with Sam there and, with this thought in his mind, he said, 'I do like it here, don't you?'

9

Dawn was breaking as Raymond parked the Bentley in one of the car parks in Penzance. He took the two bags from the boot of the car and, with Joanna, walked to a restaurant that overlooked the harbour. While they waited for it to open, they looked at the boats bobbing up and down at their moorings.

At last, the restaurant opened and Raymond treated Joanna to a hearty breakfast. Then they walked to the pier head and purchased two return tickets to the Isles of Scilly. They boarded the ship that was waiting there and after a short time the ship began to move.

The first attempt to manoeuvre the Scillonian from the pier head resulted in scratching the paint on her stern, but the second attempt proved more fruitful and within ten minutes she was underway, her engines under full power thrusting the ship forward towards the open sea.

Raymond and Joanna whiled away the journey sitting on deck enjoying an ice cream and now, after a few hours, they were watching from the upper deck and could see the Islands of Scilly on the horizon. Another half hour passed and the Scillonian manoeuvred close to her moorings in the harbour of Saint Mary's.

They disembarked and found a water taxi that would take them to the neighbouring islands. Raymond had arranged to rent a holiday cottage on the island of Tresco so, as the small boat stopped at the jetty, they were met by an island attendant and accompanied to their cottage. They were treated as though they were holidaymakers. Raymond knew the island well, having been there many times before, but he didn't mention this to their guide. It was only a short walk to the cottage and when they arrived, Raymond thanked the attendant, and they went inside.

After looking around the cottage they decided to walk to the small inn that was situated at the centre of the island. Tresco is only one and a half miles long and half a mile wide, there were no cars to avoid, only agricultural tractors and bicycles. The fresh sea air smelled so good to them, and the morning sun was warming as they continued their walk.

'It's a beautiful place,' remarked Joanna, 'have you been here before?'

'Many times,' Raymond answered. 'Come with me; let me show you the beach before we go to the inn.'

It wasn't far from the cottage, 'Look at that,' he said, 'isn't that beautiful?'

The sand was a silvery white and too hot to touch because of the penetrating sun in a cloudless sky.

'You couldn't walk barefoot on it,' said Raymond. The blue, crystal-clear sea rushed at the sand and as though it had changed its mind midway, slipped back where it had come from. They turned away from the glorious beach and continued their walk to the inn.

When they entered the inn, the atmosphere was warm and welcoming. There was a big fishing net draped across the rafters, caught up in it were many sea urchins and two or three coloured glass witch balls.

The inn was packed with nautical memorabilia

on every surface. On the wall directly opposite the door was a wooden ship's steering wheel with a brass core; on the wall opposite the bar were two life belts with 'C. Spray' written on them and a large lobster pot had been placed at one end of the bar. But what caught Joanna's eye were six photographs hanging behind the bar, all pictures of a ship. The inn was busy so Joanna waited until the barman came close enough, and asked, 'Are they all the same ship? They do look alike.'

'No,' the barman answered, 'they're all called the Scillonian, but not the one you must have travelled on today. These are the ones that have been lost trying to reach Saint Mary's harbour. Many ships, even old galleons, have sunk off the coast here with their treasures intact. We get a lot of divers here in the summer,' he spoke with an Australian accent. 'Now, what can I get you?' he asked.

'I see on your menu you have something called a green beer, what's in it?'

'Half beer, half lemonade and a shot of crème de menthe, that's what makes it green,' he said smiling.

'Two please,' she said, then she turned to Raymond, 'It's very crowded in here, do you mind if we go outside with our drinks?' The barman returned with their drinks and Raymond paid him.

'Just before you go,' Raymond asked, 'can you tell me if you have seen Captain Journal around anywhere?'

'He hasn't been in today, but he'll be in later, with his first and second mates, Joe and Ginger.'

'Two mates,' said Raymond.

'Yeah, if you listen to them, they have sailed the seven seas together. I'm not keen on those two though, they're bad ones, real bad ones.'

'Thanks,' said Raymond, then the barman was gone and Joanna and Raymond pushed their way past the people in the crowded bar. A group of teenagers arrived and one started to play a guitar; soon the air was filled with sea shanties. A bottle of red wine arrived and the singers' glasses were filled.

Joanna and Raymond were glad to get outside and Joanna sipped her green beer, 'It's minty and fizzy,' she said, 'but very nice.' If they had stayed and looked a little further into the crowded inn they would have seen a group of men huddled in a corner, watching them: Louis La Ronde and his two henchmen.

La Ronde turned angrily to Victor, 'Did you tell him about Journal?'

'I had to, Boss; he was going to kill me.'

'And you think that I won't?' he replied coldly. 'But we can take advantage of his persistence. What better place to dispose of him? There are accidents all the time on these islands.'

As Louis La Ronde was explaining the new plan to his men, two men approached their table and interrupted the conversation. One was well built with ginger hair and dressed in black, the other was bigger than the first, also dressed in black with a black beard that partially concealed a scar on his face.

'You La Ronde?' asked the man with the beard.

'Who wants to know?'

'The Captain wants to see you,' he said.

'Where's the Captain?'

The bearded man jerked his head in the direction of the bar. 'Over there, wearing the Captain's hat.'

As the big man standing at the bar turned to face

La Ronde, he revealed the words 'Sea King' in white, written across the front of his black polo neck jumper.

He walked slowly to the table and stood between his two mates. He paused, and then he asked, 'Have you got it?'

'Yes, but not here, there may be a slight problem,' answered La Ronde.

'Problems are not part of the deal.' Captain Journal paused again to think, and then asked, 'What problem?'

'One man,' said Louis La Ronde, 'Raymond Spade. He is trying to stop me delivering the diamond to you.'

'Is he?' He said to Ginger, one of his mates, 'Tell the barman to let Spade know that I'll be receiving the diamond tomorrow morning at ten, on the gun platform at Cromwell's Castle.'

'Yes, Captain.' The man with the ginger hair went to the bar and spoke to the barman. He soon returned and said, 'The trap is set.'

'How do you know the barman will tell him?' asked La Ronde.

'Everyone talks to the barman; don't you talk to your barber? It's the same thing,' answered Captain Journal knowingly.

Then he said to Joe and Ginger, 'I want both of you to meet Spade at Cromwell's Castle in the morning, where he'll have a fatal accident. Do you get my meaning?'

'Yes, Captain,' was the answer.

'La Ronde,' Journal said quietly, 'I will meet you here tomorrow afternoon when Spade has been taken care of. You will bring the diamond and I will pay you for it.' The men all sat at the table, eating, drinking, talking and waiting for Raymond to return to the bar. In time he did, to return the beer glasses, and they watched as the barman spoke to him casually for a few moments. As Raymond moved away from the bar, the barman glanced over at them; the message had been passed on as planned.

Raymond left the inn with Joanna and they walked slowly back to the cottage in silence, enjoying the afternoon sun and sea air, both thinking their own thoughts. They entered the cottage and while Raymond gave some thought as to how to intercept the handover, Joanna prepared an evening meal, as she did he told her about the information he'd received from the barman.

'When will you go to Cromwell's Castle?'

'I thought I'd start out early, about eight, I want to get there before Captain Journal arrives.' Then Joanna asked what Raymond was dreading to hear her say.

'Can I come with you?'

'I don't think that's a good idea, it'll be dangerous,' he replied.

'I promise I won't get in your way, and if things don't go according to your plan, I may even be helpful.'

Raymond rose from the table and held out his hand. 'Let's go and take a look at the sea,' he said. Joanna came close to him and he put his arm around her shoulders. Together they left the cottage.

It was dark outside; the moon and stars were the only source of light. They walked along the small path towards the beach. Many tiny bats filled the night sky and they had to duck on a few occasions to avoid being hit by the small creatures.

They passed through sand dunes dressed in

patches of long thin grass that swayed in the cool night breeze. On the beach, the now darkened sea licked at the silver white sand that reflected the moonlight. There were rocks at both ends of the beach; they looked rugged and dangerous from where they were standing. Raymond took off his jacket and spread it out on the sand.

'Sit down, Jo,' he said. She sat upon Raymond's jacket and he sat on the sand next to her.

'It is truly beautiful here, Ray,'

'Yes, it is. I like the way the locals use boats the same way we use cars. Everything seems so much slower here on the Islands. This way of life would be good for us.'

'Are you thinking of staying here?'

'No, I couldn't do that, though I could be tempted.' Just then a meteor streaked silently across the clear sky.

'Oh look, a shooting star!' exclaimed Joanna, 'Make a wish, Ray.'

'I did, didn't you?' he asked.

'It was all too fast, it was gone by the time I asked you if you had made a wish,' she looked into his eyes and asked, 'what did you wish for?'

'I wished that one day I could ask you to marry me.' She moved so that she could put her arms around him and whispered, 'Not now, but one day.' They stayed until it was late into the night, happy in each other's company. There were no more shooting stars although they watched the sky, just in case there was another wish to be granted.

'We must get some rest,' Raymond said, as he helped Joanna to her feet. He picked up his jacket and brushed the sand from it, then they turned their backs on the beautiful sight and walked slowly back to the cottage. The night had passed peacefully, though Raymond's wish had played over and over in Joanna's mind.

The following morning, when he opened his eyes the sun was spreading light and life onto a new day. He looked at his watch and then lazily dragged himself out of bed. He was surprised that he had slept so well, better than he had for a long time. He thought over what he had said to Joanna on the beach last night, and was happy that he had told her what he had been feeling almost since the first time he had met her. They both enjoyed breakfast, and afterwards started the walk to Cromwell's Castle.

The path was narrow and rocky. On their right, beyond the bushes were tropical plants of numerous colours, grass and large boulders. To their left were rocks and a long drop to the crystal blue sea below. The boats and yachts moored beyond the rocks looked splendid and somehow unreachable in the morning sun.

They walked on admiring the pleasant view as the path wove its way along the top of the cliffs and over a high ridge. It was from the top of this ridge that they first saw the ruins of Cromwell's Castle. But, as they looked up, overlooking it from the top of the high land of the Island, were the ruins of King Charles' Castle. They walked on, Raymond estimated about half a mile before arriving at their destination.

Cromwell's Castle stood on a small peninsula that reached out into the sea. The main structure was circular in shape, but small for a castle. They approached cautiously. Twenty stone steps led from the ground to an archway. They climbed them silently.

When they reached the top, they stepped inside to find themselves in a round stonewalled room, and there was another set of steps leading down into darkness.

'Stay here,' said Raymond. He ventured down three or four steps staring into the blackness. As his eyes adjusted to the darkness, he took his little torch from his pocket and looked down into the pit. He soon realised that there was no way out except by the steps he was standing on. The floor of the pit was covered with sand and there was obviously no-one there. He put his torch back into his pocket and made his way back to the circular room.

As he entered Joanna said, 'Look Ray, there are more steps here, looks like they lead to another archway.' They peered up the steps and they could see blue sky, so they climbed the steps and passed through the archway. Once outside they were standing on a gun platform. There were two big cannons pointing over a small wall that made up the battlements. Raymond looked down the sights of both cannons and found them to be trained in the same place, the centre of the harbour mouth.

'Of course,' he said.

'What is, of course?' asked Joanna.

'The sights on the cannons are both trained on the centre of the harbour mouth; gunships would have to be in the centre to enter the harbour, they wouldn't have the draft to get in any other way.'

'And this means something?' said Joanna.

'It means that these cannons would blow them out of the water if they were enemy ships.'

'Oh,' muttered Joanna as she raised her eyebrows.

10

They turned away from the cannon to explore the rest of the Castle, but instead were confronted by two men, both very well built, one was dark haired with a full beard, the other was clean shaven with ginger hair. They walked slowly towards Raymond and Joanna. The Herkimer crystal around Joanna's neck started to vibrate. She touched Raymond's arm, 'This is not good,' she whispered.

'Good morning,' Raymond greeted them.

'Is it?' asked the ginger headed man.

'It's not raining...' smiled Raymond as he pointed at the sun. The two men came closer and Raymond stepped in front of Joanna.

'This is private property,' said the dark-haired man, in an accusing manner.

'Is it?' answered Raymond. 'Then we'll leave.'

'You can't leave just like that, you'll have to pay for being here,' the ginger haired man said, and he pulled a cosh from his coat pocket. He went for Raymond, his arm raised to strike him across the head. Raymond side-stepped, blocked, and brought his hand down on the man's wrist in a vicious chop. Something cracked and the cosh fell to the floor. The ginger haired man let out a cry of pain, followed by vehement cursing.

The dark-haired bearded man was next. As far as Raymond could see, he was not armed but he came at him his arms swinging violently. A perfectly executed kick landed in his stomach. The force propelled him back along one of the cannons and over the little wall.

Raymond knew he would fall to his death and tried to reach out to him, he managed to grab his arm, but was hit on the head from behind with the cosh.

Raymond fell to the ground, hitting his head on one of the four metal wheels that supported the cannon. He lay still, totally senseless, between the two big guns. The ginger haired man moved to the edge of the gun platform and peered over one of the cannons. His fears were confirmed: the bearded man, Joe, was lying on the rocks below. He turned to face Joanna, 'He's dead,' he said. He moved away from the edge of the gun platform and kicked Raymond in the back as he passed him.

'You and your friend will pay for this.' He left Joanna and began walking away from Cromwell's Castle holding his wrist as he went.

Raymond began to stir. He opened his eyes and was aware of a throbbing pain in his head and back. Then a shadow shielded his eyes against the strong dazzling sun.

'Ray? Oh Ray! I thought you were dead.'

'I thought I was too,' he said as he struggled to his feet.

'The ginger haired man is gone,' she paused, 'the other man fell over the wall, I think he's dead.'

A little blood trickled down the side of Raymond's face so Joanna gave him a handkerchief. He placed it to the side of his head and put his arm around her shoulders. Together they walked from the gun platform, through the circular room and down the stone steps. Once outside, Joanna helped Raymond to sit down on the soft green grass and they looked out over the rugged rocks and blue sea.

'That feels a little better.'

'Do you think that you can walk?'

'Yes, I think so.' She helped him to his feet and they began the long walk back to the cottage.

'I tried to save the man that attacked me, but I must have missed my footing.'

'No, the ginger haired man stopped you. You would have saved him, but he hit you from behind.'

'I bet that's not the way La Ronde will hear it.'

'I don't think they were La Ronde's men; they're not the men that he's sent after us before.'

Raymond was leaning more on Joanna than he would have liked, but he didn't have much choice. He didn't say anything, but he was still quite dizzy. They walked along the dusty path, the sun still shining and the heat making it difficult for Raymond to keep going. He was glad that Joanna was with him and he continued to lean on her until they reached the cottage.

'I think you need to sleep for a while,' Joanna said as she guided him up the stairs. She helped him onto the bed and closed the curtains.

'I'll bring something for the headache, and then you try to sleep.'

She left his room and went to the first aid cabinet in the bathroom. When she returned, he was already asleep, so she left him. The sleep would do him good. With nothing else to do, she left the cottage and went to look at the beautiful sandy beach, as she had done the night before when Raymond wished upon a shooting star.

* * *

It was late afternoon when Ginger arrived at the inn. He walked into the bar and over to a table where his boss, Captain James Journal and Louis La Ronde were sitting with two other men. When they saw Ginger, Captain Journal asked, 'Is it done?'

'No,' Ginger replied. Before he had time to say anything else, he was asked, 'Why?'

Ginger waited a moment and then answered, 'Spade is still alive,' he paused, 'and Joe is dead.' Although Captain Journal gave the impression of being a hard sea captain, he was shaken by the news of his first mate. Joe had been his most trusted man of the two.

'What happened?'

'Spade kicked him in the stomach and he fell off the gun platform onto the rocks below.'

'Are you sure he was dead?'

'He would have died from the fall and the tide will have carried his body out to sea by now,' Ginger answered.

Captain Journal turned to La Ronde. 'Where is the diamond?'

La Ronde produced a small soft chamois leather bag and placed it on the table. Captain Journal picked it up and extracted the Snowflake Diamond. He examined it carefully. When he was satisfied, he replaced it back into the leather bag and pushed the bag into his pocket.

'I'll make sure Spade won't come looking for this,' stated La Ronde.

'He has already killed one of my men!' shouted Captain Journal.

'Not so loud, people are listening.'

'I will buy the diamond, but I want that girl he was with too.'

Louis La Ronde spoke to his two henchmen, 'Find

Joanna Sommers and bring her here.' Oliver and Vincent rose from the table and left the inn.

'They will bring her back, if you are willing to wait,' said La Ronde. Captain Journal turned his attention to Ginger, 'Why did you fail?'

'He broke my wrist and he killed Joe, I couldn't fight him with one hand.'

'Take a boat and go back to St Mary's, get your wrist set,' ordered the Captain. Ginger said nothing and left the inn.

* * *

Joanna had spent about an hour just watching the swell of the sea, and the sand dunes with their long swaying grass. The light was fading when she decided to go back to the cottage. As she left the beach she saw two figures walking towards her in the darkness. By the time she recognised them, it was too late.

'Good evening, Miss Sommers. Don't try and run, I don't want to cut you to pieces.' She stopped walking. One of the men was holding a Bowie knife.

'Where is your friend, Spade?'

'He went back to St Mary's,' she replied.

'That was careless of him to leave you here, alone. You're coming with us; Mr. La Ronde wants to see you.'

Joanna knew who the men were, the Herkimer crystal around her neck was vibrating in their presence.

'Oliver and Victor, or should I call you the Harlequin?' They didn't answer her.

'I'm right, aren't I?' There was still no answer.

'So, the Bowie knife is your weapon of choice, is

it, Victor? As I recall, Ray took the last one away from you.'

The two men were trying not to let Joanna get to them, but Victor snapped, 'I'll get my knife back, and I'll put it between Spade's shoulder blades.'

'So, you are going to stab him in the back. Are you still afraid to face him?' taunted Joanna.

'And I'll take my gun from your friend too, and when I do, I just might leave a bullet in him,' added Oliver.

They walked from the beach, Victor putting the Bowie knife out of sight, under his coat. They continued to walk to the inn and, on their arrival, Joanna was taken to Louis La Ronde's table. He was pushing a big bulging brown envelope into his inside pocket, concluding his deal with Captain Journal.

'Thank you, Captain. This is what I like, cash on delivery.' Louis La Ronde rose from the table, 'Good doing business with you. If you ever want anything else, and I mean anything, I can obtain it for you,' then he added, 'at a price.'

He looked at his men, and Joanna standing between them. 'Time to go,' he said abruptly. The three men left the inn, and left Joanna to her fate.

Captain Journal stared at her, 'Your friend killed one of my men,' he stated.

'No, he didn't.'

The Captain looked into her blue eyes for a moment. 'What is your version of events?'

Joanna sat down at the table.

'The big man with the beard tried to hit Ray and so Ray kicked him first.'

'Go on.'

'The man was falling backwards, along the

cannon and over the wall, Ray tried to grab his arm but the ginger haired man hit him with his cosh and Ray lost his grip. Your man fell onto the rocks below. Ray lay unconscious for a few minutes. By the time he woke up, the ginger haired man had gone.'

'I want Raymond Spade,' said Captain Journal, 'and you are going to stay with me until he comes to get you.'

'I'm not staying with you; in fact, I'm leaving right now.' Joanna stood up and attempted to leave. Captain Journal grabbed her wrist and pulled a gun from his pocket.

'Sit down!' he shouted. The other guests looked around to see what all the commotion was about.

'Help! Help me!' shouted Joanna, looking desperately around the inn for someone who would help her. But when the guests saw the gun, they fled.

* * *

It was dark outside when Raymond awoke. He called, 'Jo?' but there was no reply. The headache had cleared and, apart from a pain in his back, he felt alright. He went down the stairs and called 'Jo?' again but there was still no reply.

When he was sure that she was not in the cottage, he decided to go to the inn. It was starting to get dark and he hastened his step. As he approached, he was aware of a lot of people coming out of the building. Raymond stopped a man and asked what was happening. 'There's a man with a gun, he's holding a girl in there.' In his haste to get into the inn Raymond didn't notice that among the crowd, were Louis La Ronde and his two henchmen. When they saw Raymond, they pushed their way back into the inn.

Raymond burst into the inn and was confronted by Captain Journal. He was holding a gun close to Joanna's head.

'Let her go!' said Raymond firmly.

'Are you Spade?'

'Yes, I am. What do you want?'

'You! You killed one of my men this morning at Cromwell's Castle,' Captain Journal said accusingly.

'If your other man hadn't stopped me, I would have saved him.'

'My other man has gone to have his wrist set at the hospital.' As he said this, he moved the gun away from Joanna and motioned in the air, in the direction of St Mary's.

That was all Raymond needed. He grabbed the Captain's wrist, twisted it hard and the gun fell to the floor, In his present position, he was standing with his back to the Captain and so he finished his move with his left elbow to the ribs, hitting the air out of his opponent's lungs. As the Captain doubled up, Raymond used his left arm again. This was more of a reflex action as the back of his clenched fist struck the Captain between his eyes. He fell back into one of the chairs totally unconscious. Raymond was about to pick up the gun that the Captain had dropped when a voice said, 'Leave it.'

Raymond looked up to see Louis La Ronde holding a jewel encrusted flintlock duelling pistol, and his two henchmen. 'You keep getting in my way, don't you?'

'If it makes you feel any better, I wish we'd never met in Austria,' remarked Raymond.

'Strangely enough, I wish that too. You see, now we will have to kill you and any witnesses.' He turned to his henchmen, 'I want him dead,' he looked at Joanna, 'and Miss Sommers. Do it, and do it now!'

Raymond knew he had to move fast, he watched as Victor produced the Bowie knife from inside his coat, but to Raymond's surprise, he gave it to Oliver. Then he put his hand into his pocket and produced the shiny knuckleduster with two protruding points. He fitted it to his right hand.

'Time to die, Mr. Spade,' said Louis La Ronde as he stepped back to give his men more room. The two men came at Raymond together, but Oliver was the first one to strike with the knife. He slashed at Raymond from right to left at chest height, as the knife passed in front of Raymond, he delivered such a focused, penetrating punch to Oliver's liver that the man just dropped the knife and fell to the floor holding his side.

'He's going to need a doctor,' Raymond said as he looked for an opening against Victor, who had adopted a boxer's stance. The flash of silver on Victor's right hand drew Raymond's attention to the double pronged knuckle duster.

'Surely not Queensberry rules, you surprise me, Victor.' Raymond knew how to deal with a boxer. Working on the idea that a leg has more reach than an arm, he went for a straight kick that landed with great force between Victor's legs, lifting him into the air. He doubled up and fell on his knuckleduster. He didn't cry out, he just groaned, so Raymond assumed he had not fallen on the two sharp points.

'Very impressive, Mr. Spade, but I doubt that not even you can avoid a bullet.' La Ronde levelled the flintlock pistol at Raymond. 'It's true what they say, if you want something done, do it yourself.'

Raymond knew that to aim a flintlock pistol with any accuracy was notoriously difficult. He took two or three paces back and watched La Ronde warily. Suddenly, Joanna appeared behind him and smashed a very good bottle of brandy over La Ronde's head. La Ronde crumpled to the floor. Raymond picked up the knife and the gun from the floor and crossed the room to Captain Journal; he searched his pockets until he found the chamois leather bag and said, 'I'll return it for you.' There was no reply from the still unconscious Captain.

'Should we take La Ronde's flintlock pistol?' asked Joanna.

'No,' replied Raymond. 'If he wants to use a gun, a single shot will give whoever he is shooting at a chance, especially if he misses. It takes time to reload a flintlock.' He smiled and put his arm around her. 'Come on, Jo, it's time to go home.'

Together they left the inn and walked back to the cottage. The night air was refreshing with the fragrance of sea salt and the moon and stars shone brightly in a clear sky. It felt just as if they were on holiday and all too soon they were back at the cottage. Inside, Raymond took the soft leather bag from his pocket. Taking the Snowflake Diamond from it, he placed it on the table.

'It's beautiful, Jo,' he whispered staring at the light refracting through the diamond.

'Not another one like it in the entire world,' she said, 'and it will sparkle so much better in daylight.'

'When we get back, we must deliver it to Scotland Yard.' Then he added, 'Thank you, Jo.'

'For what?' she asked.

'The brandy. La Ronde was right, I'm not fast

enough to dodge a bullet.'

'That's why I hit him; I didn't think you were either.' He put his arm around her and kissed her forehead.

It was early the following morning when they packed their bags to go home. Raymond had wrapped the knife and the gun in a towel and placed it at the bottom of his bag and Joanna had put the chamois leather bag that contained the Snowflake Diamond into the bottom of her shoulder bag.

They left the cottage and walked slowly to the beach. It really was a beautiful place. The waves with their white caps rushed in to meet the silver sand. The long blades of green grass swayed gentle in the sea breeze. It was truly a wonderful place.

'Will we come back one day?' Joanna asked.

'Yes, I would like that very much,' Raymond paused, 'There is more to us than just this beautiful place, isn't there Jo?'

'Yes,' she answered, 'much more.' He kissed her softly and then took her hand. They left the sandy beach behind them and went in search of a water taxi. It didn't take long to find one and they boarded it. The sea was calm and the voyage short. It was still early when they arrived on the Island of St Mary's. The Scillonian had not yet arrived and so they went in search of some breakfast, and then a police station.

11

They entered the police station to be greeted by a sergeant at the desk who said, 'Good morning, how can I help you?'

'I have reason to believe that a man went into the sea near Cromwell's Castle off the Island of Tresco yesterday morning,' stated Raymond.

'And how do you know this?'

'I was there I tried to save him from falling from the gun platform, but then I was hit from behind and became unconscious. I didn't see him go over, but I don't know how he could not have fallen.'

The officer looked up from his notes and seemed unsure how to proceed for a moment. 'Thank you for reporting this incident. We get lots of missing person's reports and the people concerned usually turn up sooner or later. I will make a note of it, but I wouldn't worry too much about it. Can I just take your name?'

'Yes, it's Raymond Spade, and we are hoping to sail on the Scillonian this afternoon back to Penzance.'

'Please wait here for a moment; I'd like you to see Inspector Gibbins before you leave.' He left his desk for a few minutes, returning with another man.

'Mr. Spade, I am Inspector Gibbins.' A well-built man wearing a dark suit and holding a mug of hot coffee in one hand, he reached out to Raymond with his other, 'I'm pleased to make your acquaintance.' Raymond took his hand and introduced Joanna, 'This is Miss Sommers.'

Inspector Gibbins made his way out from behind

the desk and said, 'You want to report a missing person?'

'That is correct,' confirmed Raymond.

'A man fell from the gun platform at Cromwell's Castle on Tresco Island. That is what you told my Sergeant.'

'Yes, I did.'

'Do you have any idea who he was?'

'I think he worked for Captain James Journal,' answered Raymond.

'James Journal, he's calling himself Captain now, is he? He is a really bad lot.'

'He has been trying to buy the Snowflake Diamond,' stated Raymond.

'You mean you know about the theft of the Snowflake Diamond?'

'Only the news reports,' Raymond answered.

'Seeing as you know about Journal trying to buy the Snowflake Diamond, I must ask if you know who is selling it?'

'I do.' There was a paused.

'I must ask for a name,' Inspector Gibbins said impatiently.

'Alright, I can give you a name. The man you are looking for is Louis La Ronde, last seen on Tresco, at the inn.'

'Can you give me any more information?'

'He has at least two henchmen, and he owns the Second-Hand Antique Shop in London. He boasts that he can obtain anything for anyone who will pay, and his prices are very high.'

Then Raymond asked, 'Are you allowed to tell me how he was able to commit a robbery like this?'

'The details are not available for the public, and

only top men of the police force have been made aware of the details. The Snowflake Diamond was stolen from a security van on the motorway. It was well done. Not that I am condoning it. I just mean it was ingenious to use three police cars to stop the van. No passing motorist would think that it was a robbery. The diamond was replaced with a copy and the theft was only discovered once it reached its destination. The guards that were with the van were treated politely and with courtesy. They didn't suspect the men who were dressed in police uniforms to be anything else than policemen doing their job. Somehow, they opened the safe and exchanged a copy for the real Snowflake Diamond. I only know about this because I am in charge of the Islands, and you, Mr. Spade, are the best lead to come to light so far. Is there anything else that you can tell me about La Ronde or Journal?'

Raymond shook his head, 'Sorry, Inspector, nothing else,' he said, knowing that the Snowflake Diamond was at the bottom of Joanna's shoulder bag.

'Is there a place where I can reach you?' asked Inspector Gibbins.

'Yes, I live at The Five Pines on Exmoor. If there is anything I can do, just let me know.'

'Thank you, Mr. Spade. I will have James Journal watched. As I said, he is a very unsavoury character.'

'Thank you, Inspector, the secret of the Snowflake is safe with me, and thank you too, Sergeant.' Raymond left the police station with Joanna. Once outside Joanna asked in a whisper, 'Why didn't you give the Snowflake to Inspector Gibbins?'

'I would like Louis La Ronde to be in police custody before I give away our only bargaining chip.'

'He won't come after us now, would he?'

'After what happened in the inn yesterday. I would come after us.'

'I see what you mean. He knows we took the Snowflake.'

'We will give it a day or two and if there is no retaliation from La Ronde, we can carry out are original plan and deliver it to Scotland Yard in London.' Joanna was happy with this and they walked slowly through the streets of Saint Mary's at last arriving at the harbour. But, standing with two other men at the place where the Scillonian would dock, was Captain Journal.

'This could be a problem,' said Raymond. 'They are doubtless looking for us. Here, Jo, take my bag and the keys for the Bentley. I'll walk close to them and we'll see if they make contact. If I don't come back by the time the Scillonian is due to sail, go aboard and, when you get back to Penzance, take the Bentley and go to The Five Pines, check on your Uncle Rubin and Sam, make sure your uncle is safe.'

'I will but, till then, I'll wait here for you,' answered Joanna.

Raymond left her and walked to the sea wall where the Scillonian would dock, deliberately passing close to Captain Journal and the other two men. They were both wearing black thick woollen jumpers with Sea King sewn onto them in white. Then Raymond noticed a fishing boat moored close to the sea wall, it bore the name, Sea King.

'Mr. Spade,' called Captain Journal, 'I think you should join us on a little diving trip. I won't take the gun out of my pocket, but I will shoot you if you resist. Go aboard the Sea King.'

Raymond boarded the fishing boat and was soon joined by Captain Journal and his two men.

'Where are we going?'

'Out to sea, to Gilstone rock. We are going to dive on HMS Association. You have dived before?' queried the Captain.

'I know how to use an aqualung,' replied Raymond.

The boat's engine was started and the Sea King sailed out of the harbour. Joanna watched the fishing boat until she couldn't see it any more. Then she went back to the police station and told Inspector Gibbins what had happened.

'Leave it with me,' he had said, so she returned to the harbour and waited in hope for the Sea King to return, but it didn't. She did notice a police helicopter rise into the sky and head out to sea.

'I hope it is carrying a guardian angel. Ray is going to need one,' she whispered to herself.

Then there was more activity in the harbour as the Scillonian arrived, and the day trippers disembarked to spend some time on the Islands. Joanna mingled with the sightseers until it was time to go back to the mainland.

She boarded the ship with the other passengers and made herself comfortable for the voyage back to Penzance. The journey on the Scillonian was smooth as the ship was fitted with stabilizers; she was designed to be able to enter Saint Mary's harbour without hitting any of the many underwater rocks.

It was twilight, early evening, when the ship docked at Penzance and the passengers disembarked. Joanna, although hungry, didn't stop for anything to eat. She went to the car park and collected the

Bentley. The car was automatic and not at all what she was used to, but she did have to admit that it was far more comfortable than her Alfa Romeo.

As the evening changed into night, she drove on until she was travelling across Exmoor and, very soon, she parked the Bentley in the grounds of The Five Pines, next to the Ferrari. She grabbed her shoulder bag and left Raymond's bag in the car. She noticed another car in the driveway, a black Mercedes, but she didn't stop to think who it might belong to, she just continued into the big house. She called, 'Uncle Rubin,' as she climbed the stairs, unaware that the Herkimer crystal around her neck had begun to vibrate. As she entered the lounge she was surprised to see none other than Louis La Ronde and his two henchmen. Rubin and Sam were sitting on the large settee.

Oliver, the larger of the two men had picked up his Smith & Wesson from the shelf above the fireplace. He was waving it around making all kind of threats as to what he was going to do when he caught up with Raymond Spade.

But when Victor saw Joanna he produced a Bowie knife from inside his coat and began waving it in front of her face. 'Do you remember this?' He paused, 'Do you remember me?'

Joanna stepped back saying, 'Yes, yes I do, you are the Harlequin, you buried Ray alive in the graveyard, and, yes, your Bowie knife frightened me. But not anymore, Ray has taken it away from you more than once and he will do it again.'

Victor grabbed her shoulder bag and flung it across the room. This was more than enough for Rubin, he rose to his feet and drew his sword stick.

'Hey, you!' he shouted, as he brought his sword down on Victor's back like a whip. Victor turned towards Rubin and tried to slash him with his knife. To his surprise, Rubin moved towards him and in a lunging motion scratched Victor's hand with the point of his sword. He let rip a stream of oaths and tried to advance on Rubin again.

Sam, seeing his opportunity, rose from the settee and went for Oliver who was still waving his gun around and shouting. Sam had always fancied himself as a boxer and so he barged into Oliver, hitting the gun from his hand. Oliver didn't know what hit him. Sam was big, black and very strong. He took up a standard boxing stance and then rained three or four left jabs into Oliver's face, finishing with a right cross. Oliver lay unconscious at Sam's feet. Sam went to pick up the gun but a voice said, 'Leave it.'

Sam looked at La Ronde. He was standing in all his finery next to the bay window and he was holding a flintlock pistol in his hand. 'Sit down,' he gestured with his pistol in the direction of the settee, Sam looked La Ronde in the eyes and slowly sat down. 'I am interested in how this will work out, a Bowie knife against a sword.'

'Rubin is an old man, this is hardly a fair fight,' protested Sam with concern.

Victor continued to slashed with his knife, but Rubin was always ahead in his strategy, anticipating the next move, and continued to prick Victor's knife hand with the point of his sword stick. It wasn't long before Victor's hand was covered in blood and he had difficulty holding his knife. It had become like a very slippery piece of soap. Rubin, very skilfully placing the point of his sword between the guard of the knife and

Victor's hand, rotated his sword two or three times and the knife fell to the floor. Rubin seized his advantage and placed the point of his sword at Victor's throat.

'The sword is the weapon of a gentleman, and that, sir, you will never be.'

'That will be enough,' La Ronde said, his pistol now pointing at Rubin.

'I should run you through,' he said, then he looked at the pistol, 'but maybe not today.' He moved away from Victor and picked up his empty stick and, just before he sat down on the settee, he wiped the tip of his sword on Victor's sleeve, then replaced his sword into its stick.

'Looks Victorian,' remarked La Ronde.

'Yes, around about 1888, the days of Jack the Ripper,' replied Rubin. 'It still works very well, despite its age.'

'As do you,' added La Ronde.

Victor bound a handkerchief around his hand and picked up his knife. He crossed the room to where Joanna was and passed the blade close to her face. 'See, boss, she does remember,' he said proudly. 'Where is the Snowflake Diamond?' he demanded, as the knife passed even closer to Joanna's face.

'You are no Harlequin,' she said. 'You are just a hired thug and not a very good one. My uncle could have ended your life here, today.' Victor felt his temper rising and taking his knife by the blade he hit her on the side of the head with the handle and she fell unconscious to the floor. As she did, Oliver began to stir. He sat up and cushioned his jaw. Seeing his gun on the carpet close to him, he picked it up and put it into his pocket.

Louis La Ronde had been silent while he held his

jewelled flintlock pistol on Rubin and Sam who were still sitting on the settee.

'Oliver! Get up! You are embarrassing, and you, Victor! Why do you have to overdo things? How can she tell us what she knows if she is unconscious?' he shouted.

He picked up the shoulder bag, and then walked slowly to where Joanna was lying and knelt down. He reached out and touched the golden hair that was now stained with red; there was a cut just above her eyebrow.

'Don't you have any respect for beautiful things?' He paused and looked at Victor and Oliver. 'Both of you pick her up and take her to the car.' The two men did as they were instructed and left Louis Ra Ronde, Sam and Rubin alone. Louis La Ronde threw Joanna's shoulder bag onto the settee.

'You are lucky, old man. You are alive because I want you to give Spade a message. Tell him if he wants to see Miss Sommers alive, he must bring the Snowflake Diamond to me. I will be waiting at the Hell-Fire Club Caves tomorrow night.'

'How will he know where these Hell-Fire Club Caves are?' asked Rubin.

'He will find them. If he doesn't, he won't see Miss Sommers again.'

Then Rubin spoke in a quiet voice, 'I will tell him, but you must know that if you harm her, he will hunt you down. He won't stop, not even if it takes the rest of his life. You will have nowhere to go where you'll be safe, nowhere to hide that he won't find you. Do you know how it feels to be hunted? You will live your life being afraid of shadows, second guessing yourself, looking over your shoulder and, one day you will look and he will be there, and for you it will be too late. I can tell you this because I have known men like him, when I served with the armed forces.'

La Ronde felt a flicker of doubt; part of him knew that what Rubin had said was true. A shiver of fear ran through him, he tried not to show it as he turned and left the room. Rubin and Sam watched through the window as La Ronde's black Mercedes left The Five Pines and carried Joanna away into the night.

'I will stay with you until Ray gets back,' said Sam, reassuringly.

12

Raymond had resigned himself to go with the men and now the two sailors were putting on wetsuits, flippers and aqualungs. They offered a wetsuit to Raymond and he put it on. He didn't see anyone check his aqualung, but he had no choice so he put it on. He slipped on the rubber flippers and weight belt, then he was given a face mask.

As he spat on his fingers and rubbed them around the inside of its glass, he noticed a helicopter hovering high in the sky. It was difficult to see as the pilot was keeping the craft between the fishing boat and the sun.

'Over the side, Mr. Spade,' said one of the men.

'Don't I get a knife with my wet suit?'

'No,' was the sharp reply.

Captain Journal stood in front of Raymond, 'I am going to ask you once, where is the Snowflake Diamond?'

Raymond sat on the side of the boat, 'I can honestly tell you that I don't know.'

'Then you are about to have a diving accident. They are not uncommon in these waters.' One of the men picked up a rope and pushed Raymond overboard. He was just able to put his facemask on before he hit the water.

Raymond had not done a lot of diving and it was still a novelty to him that he could suck in air while under water. The proximity of the glass of his facemask made him feel a bit claustrophobic. But everything seemed to be working and that would keep him alive, at least for now.

Then the other two men joined him in the water and they signalled him to follow them down to the wreck of the galleon below. When they realised that he wasn't following them, they swam back to him and the one carrying the rope slipped a noose around one of Raymond's flippers and pulled it tight around his ankle.

The men began to descend, and Raymond was being taken ever deeper with them. The motion of the waves above could be felt as far down as five fathoms and they continued to swim deeper, passing a rocky ledge as they did. It seemed to have been cut short and as they arrived at the wrecked galleon, they could see why. From the angle of the ship in her resting place, they could see that the ninety cannon and shot had fallen from the decks as she sank, and cut the rocky ridge on their way to the sea bed.

The two men pulled Raymond down to the wooden deck and tied the rope that was around his ankle to part of a wooden safety rail of the galleon. He suspected that there was not a lot of air left in his aqualung, but even if there was, he realised that they had only given him one air tank, when they were both wearing twin sets. He would use all his air before them.

He watched as the two men began swimming around as though they were looking for something, then he remembered that some treasure had been brought up from the Association not so long ago. He assumed that the two men that had brought him down with them were now looking for treasure, gold and silver coins, while waiting for him to run out of air.

He estimated that the old galleon must be at least two hundred years old and many divers had been here before them, but there may be something that they had overlooked.

Raymond turned his attention to the rope around his ankle, as he tried to loosen the noose, he felt the rope give, just a bit. Putting more pressure on the knot he was able to prise it apart. But just as he pulled his foot free, the two men returned. One drew a knife from its sheath on his leg and swam straight for him. Raymond moved swiftly to one side and grabbed the demand valve from the diver's mouth, then pulled his facemask off.

He looked around for the other diver, poised for another attack. Surprisingly he had gone to the first diver's aid. He watched the two men as one replaced his mouthpiece and the other dived deeper to retrieve his mate's facemask.

This was his opportunity to elude them. He swam into an open hatch and went far enough in so that his bubbles remained trapped inside the old ship, keeping out of sight, he waited and watched as the two men systematically searched for him. When they were both out of sight, Raymond started to swim to the surface.

His instinct was to swim quickly, but he knew he must not rise faster than the air bubbles around him. Occasionally he would look down but there was still no sign of them, so he continued to ascend, breaking the surface of the water just behind the Sea King.

He released his weight belt and allowed it to sink to the bottom of the sea. Then he very slowly and quietly climbed aboard, Captain Journal was nowhere to be seen. He started the engine, and it wasn't really a surprise when the Captain came rushing out of the small cabin, with a diver's knife in his hand.

'Is that the one missing from my wetsuit?'

'You thought we'd give you a knife?' sneered the Captain as he lunged at Raymond. 'I was hoping for a watery grave for you.'

Raymond put the boat into gear and opened the throttle. It pushed forward with great force, throwing the Captain off balance. Raymond grabbed his arm at the wrist, twisting it violently. The knife fell to the deck. The Captain tried to attack again, swinging his free arm wildly, but Raymond placed his arm around the Captain's neck, under his chin and, standing behind him, locked the hold with his other arm. His grip became tighter and tighter, the Captain began to feel his pulse pounding in his head. He began gasping and writhing trying to get free. When Raymond felt the Captain's body become limp, he released his grip and the Captain fell unconscious to the deck. Then he pulled the throttle back allowing the boat to slow down.

Picking up some rope that was lying on the deck he bound Captain Journal's hands behind his back. Then he set the throttle at two thirds and the fishing boat's compass on a heading of north east, for Penzance. The boat pushed its way forward through the gentle waves. It should take about two and a half hours he thought. His destination was only about 27 miles away and the sea was calm.

The voyage was uneventful. Raymond had removed the aqualung and changed the wetsuit for his own clothes. He was surprised to find his little knife and bank cards still in his pocket. Captain Journal had been forthcoming with his information about Louis La Ronde, as Raymond had threatened to throw him overboard if he didn't tell him what he knew. Most of

114

what he told him was not significant, but there was just one piece of information that Raymond was interested to hear. Louis La Ronde kept a stash of antiques in the Hell-Fire Club Caves at West Wycombe.

'How do you know this?' inquired Raymond.

'Over the years I have bought a lot of antiques from La Ronde, he took me there once. But the Snowflake Diamond is a once in a life time opportunity and you stopped me from getting it. You will pay for that, Spade.'

Raymond steered the fishing boat into Penzance harbour and moored it close to the sea wall. He looked around the harbour; the Scillonian was already at her moorings and her passengers had disembarked. Joanna would have collected the Bentley and left Penzance by now. His best guess was that she would probably be driving across Exmoor. He untied Captain Journal's hands and climbed out of the boat.

'You should go and pick up your men before they drown; it's a long swim back to Saint Mary's even if their aqualungs still have air in them. I've lost track of the time, I was down on the wreck longer than I thought.'

'You better hope I find them,' snarled Captain Journal. Raymond threw the ropes that he was holding back onto the boat and Captain Journal left the harbour almost at full throttle.

'That kind of speed must be illegal inside the harbour,' Raymond said to himself as he turned his back on the sea and went in search of the Admiral Benbow, a restaurant he had visited before. It wasn't far from the harbour and once seen, never forgotten.

On the roof lay a casting of a pirate dressed in a red hat, blue coat and black boots. In his hand he was holding a flintlock pistol.

Raymond pushed open the door and there it was in all its glory, just the way he had remembered it. He made his way through the crowded restaurant to a table and sat down. The décor all around him was made up of treasures recovered from the galleons that had been lost to the deep. Now, with diving equipment readily available, some of the treasures had been retrieved and put on display.

There were gold doubloons, pieces of eight, and other valuable coins. Goblets, sabres, daggers, swords and treasure chests were all displayed. Even the Captain's table was laid out for show. It had two crossed cutlasses and a flintlock pistol on it. Behind it, displayed on the wall hung a large ship's steering wheel and a ship's bell.

A waitress arrived at Raymond's table dressed as a serving wench of the pirate era, 'What can I get for you, sir?' she asked.

'A steak with side salad and a tankard of ale,' he answered. He took in the atmosphere of the sea-fairing theme, and when his meal arrived, he was determined to enjoy it. But then a shadow fell across his table. Slowly he looked up and there to his surprise, and relief, he recognised Inspector Gibbins.

'Inspector! Will you join me?'

'Thank you, Mr. Spade.' Inspector Gibbins sat down and a waitress came over to the table.

'Can I get you something, sir?' she asked.

'Yes please, I would like a tankard of ale and a steak, just like my friend here.'

'Friend?' inquired Raymond.

'Yes, I would like to think we are friends, or at least we can be honest with each other.' Inspector Gibbins's ale arrived and, in due course, his meal.

'We can be honest,' agreed Raymond. 'Did you have anything in particular in mind?'

The Inspector drank some of his ale and cut into his steak. 'I would like to know why you went diving with James Journal and what you discussed with him in the boat on your way back to Penzance?'

Raymond finished the last of his meal and took a long drink from his tankard.

'I went diving because I had no choice, he had a gun in his pocket. Apparently, I was going to be a diving accident. The only question he asked was if I knew where the Snowflake Diamond was.'

'Do you?'

'As I told Journal, no, I don't.'

'Then Miss Sommers took it with her,' concluded Inspector Gibbins thoughtfully. Raymond ignored that last comment.

'He told me that he has had many dealings with La Ronde and that he has a stash of antiques hidden somewhere in the Hell-Fire Club Caves at West Wycombe.'

Then Raymond asked, 'How did you know where to find me?'

'Miss Sommers came back to the police station to tell us that you had been taken out to sea by Journal and his two mates. I knew that wouldn't end well so I summoned a police helicopter to follow you. I told the pilot to keep out of sight and so he flew between the Sea King and the sun most of the time. When I saw you climb back into the boat, we let you sail out of sight and then we picked up the other two divers.

They're in a holding cell at the station on Saint Mary's. It didn't take long to fly to Penzance from Saint Mary's.'

'How long can you hold them?'

'That will depend on what charges we can bring against them.'

'How about kidnapping and attempted murder?'

'If you are willing to press charges they can be out of circulation for a long time.'

The Inspector finished the last of his meal and drained his tankard.

'I assume you'll be going home from here.'

'Yes,' replied Raymond.

'And I was right, wasn't I? Miss Sommers does have the Snowflake Diamond. Where is she taking it?'

'She's taking it back to my house, The Five Pines.'

'Do you have any transport?'

'No, I told her to take my car.'

'Then can I offer you a ride in the chopper?'

'Thank you, Inspector, that would be very welcome.' This was a surprise to Raymond.

'It comes at a price of course,' said the Inspector.

'I am guessing you don't want cash.'

'No, Mr Spade, I want the Snowflake Diamond.'

Raymond rose from the table saying, 'The meal is on me, it's the least I can do,' he paused and looked into the Inspector's eyes, 'for a friend,' he added.

'Thank you, Mr. Spade,' smiled the Inspector.

They left the restaurant and Inspector Gibbins led Raymond to some open ground where the helicopter was waiting. They climbed in and fastened their seat belts. The pilot started the engine and the rotor blades began to turn. Soon they were running to speed and the helicopter took to the sky.

The flight was brief and it wasn't long before they were hovering over The Five Pines.

'Can you put it down just there? On the turning circle of the drive,' asked Raymond. The pilot was experienced and landed the helicopter exactly were Raymond had suggested. Raymond and Inspector Gibbins jumped out of the craft and walked passed the three cars to the big oak front door.

'Yours?' said Inspector Gibbins as they passed.

'Just the Bentley and the Ferrari,' he answered. 'The Alfa Romeo is Jo's.'

'I'm glad she's here, perhaps we can discuss the diamond?'

'Let's go and get it,' said Raymond. He pushed open the big oak front door and led the Inspector into the house.

'Jo!' he called, 'Uncle Rubin! Are you here?' They heard a voice coming from upstairs. It was Rubin. 'Up here, I have been waiting for you, Ray.'

Raymond pushed the lounge door open to see Rubin and Sam sitting on the settee, his swordstick in his hand.

'Where's Jo?'

'La Ronde arrived here with his two well-built, very thick henchmen, just a few hours before Jo. They've taken her, Ray! They said if you want her back you must be at the Hell-Fire Club Caves tomorrow night, and to be sure to bring the Snowflake Diamond with you. You do have it, don't you?'

'No, I don't,' said Raymond, 'Jo, had it.'

'How can we get her back?' asked Rubin.

'Any ideas, Inspector?' enquired Raymond.

'You'll have to go to the Hell-Fire Club Caves tomorrow night as demanded, I'll arrange an armed response unit to assist in the recovery and arrest.'

'Isn't your jurisdiction on the Isles of Scilly?' asked Raymond.

'It is, but sometimes it's necessary to cover other areas,' replied the Inspector, he paused, 'now we need something to give La Ronde that resembles the Snowflake Diamond.' He looked at Raymond hopefully.

'Somehow that sounds familiar, Jo will have something I can use in her lapidary workshop,'

Raymond needed to ask the Inspector something, but it would incriminate Jo, and it could be use against her in a Court of Law. Could he trust him? He thought about all the Inspector had done to help, and he seemed to understand how they had been drawn into this whole mess.

'Did you know that Jo made the copy that replaced the Snowflake Diamond during the robbery?' The inspector remained silent.

'If it comes into your possession, would you return it to me?' Raymond asked hopefully.

'If it comes into my possession, it will be evidence.'

'If the real one comes into my possession, I'll return it to Scotland Yard, or to you, if you're around,' Raymond added.

'Thank you, Mr. Spade, I had my suspicions but I needed to hear you say it and, if I can get the copy, I'll see that you have it back.'

'That would be very generous of you, Inspector.'

The Inspector turned to leave and as he opened the door, he said, 'Good night to you all. I can see myself out.'

Raymond, Sam and Rubin watched the helicopter

slowly rise into the air from the window and in only a few minutes, it was lost to sight in the night sky.

Raymond moved from the window and picked up Joanna's shoulder bag from the settee. He pulled a few things out of it and then he produced the chamois leather bag. He opened it carefully to reveal the Snowflake Diamond.

'Did you know it was here?' asked Rubin.

'I knew where I had seen it last. Fortunately, they didn't look inside Jo's shoulder bag.'

'Both La Ronde and the one called Victor had it in their hands and both of them threw it away. Victor was in too much of a hurry to frighten her. He hit her with the handle of his Bowie knife and she was unconscious when they took her away,' related Rubin.

'I'll find her, and when I catch up to Victor… well let's just say he won't like me very much.'

Raymond, Sam and Rubin looked at the Snowflake Diamond. 'It is a beautiful thing,' remarked Rubin.

'Not another one like it in the entire world,' said Raymond, 'I was told that once by an expert.'

13

Joanna slowly opened her eyes to find herself tied to a chair by rope that cut painfully into her wrists. She was in a very expensive office-come-penthouse suite and the Herkimer Crystal around her neck was vibrating. A large wooden desk was situated in the centre of the room, and a pair of curtains hung on one of the walls. The décor of the office matched its grandeur. Sitting at the desk was a man Joanna recognised easily, dressed in his expensive clothes of lace, velvet and silks.

'La Ronde. Why am I here?'

Louis La Ronde looked at her as she spoke. 'To bring your knight in shining armour to me of course. He will pay for your freedom with the Snowflake Diamond.'

'How do you know he has it?'

'You haven't got it, and so he must have it.'

'Have you thought that maybe Captain Journal has it?' Then Joanna heard another voice from behind her.

'I've paid for it, and every time I'm about to get my hands on it, your friend Spade gets in the way.' Joanna heard footsteps behind her. Captain Journal stepped in front of her and pushed his face into hers. His breath smelled of sour rum, and he whispered, 'If I get the chance, I'm going to kill Spade tonight, and if you get in my way, I'll kill you too.'

He stood up straight, Joanna hadn't realised just how big he was. She was thankful when he went back to his chair and sat down out of her sight. But as he moved, he revealed another danger; Ginger, his wrist still in a plaster cast.

'Where are the other men? The Harlequin with the knife and the bald-headed one?'

'Have you missed them?' La Ronde laughed. 'Don't worry, they're here. They're getting ready to go and meet your friend.' Louis La Ronde rose from his desk, 'When I return, we will all go and collect the Snowflake Diamond.'

'Where are we going?' asked Joanna.

'To the Hell-Fire Club Caves, Captain Journal would like to see some antiquities that I have there.' La Ronde left the room, but Joanna knew she was not alone; she could hear Captain Journal breathing heavily behind her. When Oliver and Victor entered the room, she was never so glad to see Louis La Ronde's henchmen. They untied her and roughly pulled her out of the office and down some stairs. She was marched through a dark passage and emerged into the antiques and second-hand shop.

Joanna tried to think as she was pushed through the shop. Only minutes had passed since leaving the office and now she found herself outside in a small road. She didn't have time to call out for help before she was pushed into the back seat of a big black Mercedes. La Ronde's henchmen sat in the back, one either side of her, La Ronde sat in the driver's seat. Ginger and Captain Journal had their own car. La Ronde started the engine and moved away, Captain Journal followed them.

The cars wound their way through the London streets and away from the city. The journey was uneventful and it wasn't long before they arrived at the Hell-Fire Club Caves in West Wycombe. During the journey, Oliver had tied Joanna's hands behind her back to make her easier to control.

La Ronde opened the door and Oliver said, 'Out.' Though difficult to achieve, Joanna managed to get out of the car without any assistance, her hands still tied behind her back. Then Captain Journal and Ginger arrived in the other car.

'Ginger, stay with the car,' ordered Captain Journal. 'Warn us if anyone enters the caves.' Joanna was made to walk between Oliver and Victor, through a gothic court yard with walls of flint, to the entrance of the caves. On top of the hill above the caves was a little church with a gold ball on its roof. Next to it was the Mausoleum. Although its design made it look very picturesque, it was also used as a lookout post when the Hell-Fire Club members were in the caves.

The caves consisted of a main passage about a quarter of a mile long with various vaults and other small passages that had now been bricked up. Electric lights had been laid throughout the caves. Joanna noticed the chalk walls were covered with pick marks, made by the men of Wycombe as they dug out the caves in the 18th century.

'In,' said Oliver, and taking one arm each, Victor and Oliver pulled her into the caves. It was quite dark inside compared to the twilight of the evening sky. She definitely didn't like the situation and it seemed to be getting worse the deeper they went into the caves.

Then Oliver touched a switch and a chamber was suddenly illuminated, as were the rest of the caves. It was marked 'Robing Room'. In it was a figure of Paul Whitehead, a Steward of the Hell-Fire Club; he was dressed in Georgian clothes of the day. On his death, his Will bequeathed £50 to the club and also instructed that his heart should be cut from his body and placed in a marble urn. The urn was to be kept in the Mausoleum on top of the hill.

There was no escape. La Ronde and Journal continued deeper into the caves. Oliver and Victor followed, still holding Joanna between them. In the distance she could see what looked like a cavern and a big wooden table but no chairs. From the domed roof hung a big hook with a light bulb attached to it, illuminating the Banqueting Hall. The passageways that Joanna could see were the start of a maze of small tunnels.

They pushed her along what seemed to be the main passage towards the Banqueting Hall. Then they came upon two figures that were partially blocking the tunnel, one was a likeness of Sir Francis Dashwood, the leader of the Hell-Fire Club. The other was a figure of Benjamin Franklin supposedly being shown around the caves. They pulled Joanna passed the figures and entered the Banqueting Hall.

It was forty feet wide and sixty feet high, all dug out by hand. Even now after 200 years, the eerie atmosphere still lingered.

Situated in the walls of the Banqueting Hall were two cells both fitted with metal gates. Oliver opened one and pushed Joanna into it, locking the gate behind her. Joanna looked around her and caught sight of several stone carvings, one of which was finely worked with horns to represent the Devil.

'You are staying here until Spade shows up for you,' said Victor. Then the two men continued deeper into the caves. Fortunately, and to Joanna's relief, they left the light on. Joanna sat down on a little wooden bench and began to try to undo the knots that bound her. She struggled for a while and then she heard footsteps coming along the passage. It was Louis La Ronde and Captain Journal. As they neared the cell, they stopped and La Ronde said something to Journal that Joanna couldn't quite hear. But she did hear Journal's reply, 'I have paid you for the diamond,' he said, 'and if you shoot her now, I will pay the same amount again.'

'The same amount again?' repeated La Ronde.

'Yes, I will pay you for her death, when you hand me the Snowflake Diamond.'

'I think I can accommodate you,' agreed La Ronde.

'I want Spade to find her dead when he arrives. I want to teach him not to interfere in my affairs. One of my men is dead and two are in police custody because of him.'

The Herkimer Crystal around Joanna's neck began to vibrate violently. La Ronde stepped towards her barred cell, pausing six or seven paces away. He produced a jewel encrusted flintlock pistol from under his coat and pointed it straight at her.

'Goodbye, Miss Sommers,' he said, as he pulled the trigger. Joanna saw the hammer fall and the flash as the powder ignited, she stepped backwards until she hit the chalk wall of her cell.

'No!' she screamed.

Then out of nowhere a figure dressed in a red cloak with a tall red hat appeared in front of her. She heard the bullet ball hit the chalk wall and she fell to the floor and lay still praying there was not going to be another shot. As she lay there, she remembered why Raymond left the pistol with La Ronde when they were on the Isles of Scilly: flintlock pistols were only single shot weapons. If he wanted to shoot again, he would have to reload the gun, so she lay perfectly still. There was silence for a moment, then their footsteps moved off and, as their voices faded, she heard Journal say, 'The payment for the diamond that I gave to you on the Islands will cover payment for the girl's death, I will pay you again when you give me the Snowflake.'

'That's acceptable,' came La Ronde's reply.

Louis La Ronde and James Journal continued deeper into the caves to the Inner Temple, their purpose to examine in a bit more detail, the stash of antiques that La Ronde had concealed there.

Joanna raised her head and looked around her, but she couldn't see any signs that there had been anyone with her in the cell when the gun was fired. How could the figure in red get in and out, without opening the gate? And why hadn't La Ronde and Journal seen it?

'If you're still here, thank you, I'm not fast enough to dodge a bullet, either.'

Now that she was alone, she began working on the knots again and in only a few moments she was free. She tried to open the lock on the barred gate- unsuccessfully - so there wasn't much to do except to sit on the bench and wait for Raymond. She knew that, as long as she could hear voices echoing through the dark passageways, she was reasonably safe. What she didn't want to hear was footsteps coming back from the Inner Temple.

The Herkimer Crystal around her neck was still vibrating but less violently now; she touched it with her fingers. She knew that it had great psychic power. Suddenly a thought occurred to her. The figure in red that had saved her from the bullet ball must have been her guardian angel. The crystal's power must have summoned it. She leaned back against the wall and waited for Raymond. She knew he wouldn't leave her there, 'He'll find me, I know he will,' she whispered to herself.

14

The morning sun shone between the curtains of Raymond's bedroom window, and the memories of the night before returned to him. He dressed in his favourite brown corduroy jacket and trousers then went looking for some breakfast. Rubin was already in the kitchen with Sam when Raymond entered. He was met with the aroma of coffee and hot buttered toast.

'Almost ready. Would you like coffee or tea?' asked Rubin.

'Coffee, please,' Raymond replied.

'There's a letter for you; it arrived while you were on the Isles of Scilly,' Rubin placed Raymond's breakfast on the table next to the white envelope. Then he gave Raymond a cup of hot coffee.

'The handwriting looks like my brother's.' Raymond opened the envelope and read the letter aloud so that Rubin and Sam could hear it.

My dear friend,

I am writing to tell you that we will be coming home at the end of the month. Your cousin Richard has made all the necessary arrangements; he has been very good to us. He says if Louis La Ronde is a threat to you or us, he would like to help you to stop him. He says we would all be safer together, he is thinking of Francesca and me as his family. I hope you don't mind us returning prematurely, and that this letter finds you safe and in good health.

Your friend
M. Sommers.

Raymond sipped his coffee and asked, 'Are you and your brother close?'

'Yes, we always looked out for each other. I never married, but my brother Michael had two daughters before his wife was suddenly taken ill and died. We have always been in contact with each other, though we do live quite some distance apart. But, if he is returning from Switzerland, perhaps we should take this opportunity to live closer while we still can. I'll speak to him when he returns.'

Raymond finished his breakfast and the last of his coffee.

'If you will excuse me, I must get ready to go and get Jo back.'

'Would you like me to come with you?' asked Sam.

'Thanks, Sam, but will you stay and see that we don't get any uninvited visitors? If La Ronde thinks that I am at the Hell-Fire Club, he may send someone here.'

'I wouldn't trust him either,' said Sam, 'I will make sure nothing happens here.'

It was mid-afternoon when Raymond left for West Wycombe. Rubin came out to see him off. 'I should wish you luck,' he said.

'I'm hoping Inspector Gibbins will be there with an armed response unit. I don't want to leave anything to luck.'

'Here, you had better take this with you.' Uncle Rubin was holding the leather bag with the Snowflake Diamond wrapped inside it.

'Thanks, I'll need to give this back to Inspector Gibbins.'

'Which car will you take, Ray?'

'I think the Bentley,' he answered. The bag that he sent back with Joanna from the Isles of Scilly was still in it, and he knew that the Bowie knife and the gun were still in the bag.

'Good choice,' said Rubin. 'Exactly where are the Hell-Fire Club Caves?'

'They are on the A40 Oxford road; it'll only take a few hours to get there.' Raymond left the house. Rubin and Sam watched the Bentley drive away through the grounds of the house.

The journey to West Wycombe passed without incident and, as dusk was falling, Raymond parked the Bentley just off the road from the caves. He pushed the leather bag inside his jacket and, using the trees and bushes as cover, he made his way to the cave' entrance. He passed through the gothic courtyard with the flint walls, and followed the main passage which soon led him to the Robing Room. He was ready for anything, but he was confronted only by the figure of Paul Whitehead.

He continued through the tunnel and then entered a maze of small passages; he stayed on what seemed to be the main one. Then he saw two more figures clothed in period dress of the reign of King George III; Sir Francis Dashwood showing Benjamin Franklin around the caves in 1773. Raymond stepped cautiously passed them, the tiny pebbles grinding under his shoes as he ventured deeper, following the tunnel until he emerged into a large cavern. This was the Banqueting Hall.

He looked around and noticed the hook suspended from the ceiling. He knew that an oil lamp used to hang from it but now had been replaced with an electric bulb. There was a large table in the centre and two cells had been carved into the walls both with barred gates. Joanna was standing in one of them.

He crossed the cavern and examined the lock on the barred gate, 'Are you hurt, Jo?' he whispered. She put her arms through the bars to touch him, a small red blood stain was still visible from the blow Victor had delivered with the handle of his Bowie knife.

'This is going to take some time without the key,' he said.

'Oliver locked me in here, he'll have the key.' Then suddenly Joanna cried out, 'Ray, behind you!'

Raymond spun around to come face-to-face with Ginger; his wrist still in plaster. He produced his cosh from his pocket and stood menacingly, about three feet away.

'Come on, Ginger, you know what happened the last time you tried this.'

Ginger backed away another three feet and shouted, 'Captain Journal! Spade is here!' Raymond couldn't let Ginger sound the alarm and so he grabbed some chalk dust from the floor and threw it into Ginger's eyes. As he bent forward, rubbing his face, Raymond hit him on the back of the neck and, in less than a second, he was motionless on the chalk floor. Then he turned to Joanna, 'Look after this,' he said. However, Ginger was only stunned and saw him pass something through the bars to Joanna. She took the chamois leather bag and its precious contents.

'I'll come back for you. If you see any policemen, send them after me.' He kissed her gently through the bars and then walked noiselessly across the cavern, turned, smiled at her, and entered the tunnel.

The passage was steep and branched off to the

right and left. After a short distance they re-joined to form a triangle. The main passage continued and he followed it until he reached a round chamber which was called the Buttery. Raymond was pretty sure it was where the wine would have been kept, for one thing was certain about the Hell-Fire Club, the members would always have had plenty to drink.

Raymond walked on cautiously until he arrived at an underground river. It was named the Styx. He didn't know it but now he was 300 feet from the top of the hill and at the same level as the road at the bottom of the valley. There was a bridge spanning the river, although when the Hell-Fire Club occupied the caves, the Styx was crossed with a small rowing boat. He crossed the bridge and was now confronted with the Inner Temple.

Raymond entered and was met by Louis La Ronde, Captain Journal, Oliver and Victor.

'Come in, Mr. Spade,' said La Ronde.

'No sudden moves,' said Oliver as he took his Smith & Wesson from his pocket and trained it on Raymond.

'I want some explanations for your interest in the Snowflake Diamond.'

'Let me think… Austria, Francesca and her father, two holes in my shoulder from a self-made vampire, Rubin and Jo. I told you what would happen if you interfered with me and mine,' Raymond answered.

'Are you telling me that you are going to hunt me down and kill me?' asked La Ronde, remembering what Rubin had said, and trying to look amused.

'The only thing that will save you is a prison sentence.'

'The only thing that will save you is the Snowflake Diamond. Where is it?' demanded La Ronde.

'It won't save you from me,' added Captain Journal.

'I don't have it with me, but I know where it is.'

'That has been said so many times before, and it's not good enough! You are trying my patience.' Then Ginger entered the eerie Inner Temple.

'The girl has it,' he said, 'She tried to hide it from me, but I saw it. He gave it to her after he hit me.'

'You mean to tell me you missed with that fancy pistol you carry around with you?' shouted an outraged Captain Journal as he turned to La Ronde, 'I've already paid you and I haven't received anything yet! No diamond! And no dead girl!'

La Ronde's anger was caused by Captain Journal but aimed at Ginger. 'Your Captain told you to stay with the car and to watch for anyone entering the caves.'

'I did, and when I saw Spade enter the caves, I came to warn you.' Then La Ronde spoke to Raymond, 'You have outlived your usefulness. How do you feel about drowning in the Styx? I'm sure many have drowned here over the last two hundred years. Then we can place you and your friend in your car, I am sure it must be close by, and then deposit it into a river somewhere.'

'Come on,' said Captain Journal impatiently, 'I want to see the Snowflake.' Oliver waved his gun at Raymond, and Victor drew his Bowie knife.

'Don't you listen? Your boss said you're supposed to drown me. Only drowning didn't work out too well the last twice it was tried.'

134

'Whether you are drowned or shot will be decided after we have the diamond,' said La Ronde. They all left the Inner Temple and retraced their steps back to the Banqueting Hall. As they entered Joanna backed away from the bars of her cell.

'Take it from her!' shouted La Ronde. Oliver produced a key from his pocket and moved to the barred gate. He was just putting the key into the lock when Raymond snatched it out of his hand and threw it into the cell. Joanna picked it up.

'Oh, you are asking for it,' said Oliver as he pointed the Smith & Wesson at Raymond.

'You look very dangerous waving that gun around, I shall just take it before you shoot yourself, or me.' Raymond's hand collided with Oliver's wrist in a chopping motion. He heard something crack and knew that Oliver's wrist was broken. The gun fell to the chalk floor. Then Ginger came at Raymond, his cosh at the ready. Raymond tried the same move again, the result was quite satisfying: Ginger holding his wrist and his cosh lying at his feet.

'That's going to need a plaster cast. You're going to have a matching set.' Raymond smiled as he said it. Then it was Victor's turn. He was still waving his knife in the air.

'Victor,' Raymond said softly, 'I know you're just the hired help in all this, but you didn't have to hurt Jo like you did, and I can't forgive you for the hypnotic horror that you put her through. So, I will give you a chance: hand me the knife.'

Louis La Ronde and Captain Journal watched as the events played out. La Ronde was holding his flintlock pistol and Journal was holding a hand gun that he had taken out of his pocket. They could have fired one or both guns and put an end to Raymond but they were both curious to see just how good he was.

'Try and take it from me,' said Victor, thinking this was his chance to show La Ronde that he was worth the money he was being paid.

'Not a good choice,' said Raymond. He moved at speed with a combination of moves. His left hand pushed the knife away as his right fist hit low and deep into his opponent's stomach. The knife flew across the cavern and Raymond's knee came up and connected with Victor's nose. The force of the blow sent Victor reeling backwards, so Raymond advanced, landing the side of his hand with great force across Victor's throat. He fell onto the chalk floor gasping for breath. Then Raymond turned to face La Ronde and Journal. He saw the two guns trained on him and realised that he couldn't reach them before they were fired.

'Very impressive. You should have come to work for me,' La Ronde said, 'but it's too late now.' He levelled his antique pistol at Raymond, he smiled as he said, 'Goodbye, Mr. Spade.'

Joanna screamed, 'No!' from her cell, for she had heard La Ronde say those words before just before he tried to shoot her. Then there was another voice.

'Armed police! Place your weapons on the floor.' It was Inspector Gibbins and an armed police unit.

La Ronde and Captain Journal were reluctant to relinquish their weapons, so another warning was issued, 'Put them down, now, or we will open fire.' They laid their guns on the floor and Inspector Gibbins took control of the situation.

'Call an ambulance for these three men, and take those two into custody.' Then he walked over to

Raymond. 'Do you have the Snowflake Diamond?' he asked.

'No, Inspector, but my friend has.' They crossed the cavern and Joanna unlocked the barred gate. As she stepped out of the cell she said, 'This is for you, Inspector.' She gave the small chamois leather bag to Inspector Gibbins. He unwrapped it just enough to see the precious stone. Then he passed a package to her. 'And this one's for you; I thought you may like to have it back.'

'Thank you, Inspector,' she paused, 'can we go home now?' she asked.

'Yes. You and Mr. Spade have been of great help to us. I'll need to take statements from both of you, but that can wait for now. I know where to find you.'

'Thanks, Inspector,' Raymond said with a smile.

As Joanna and Raymond turned to leave the Hell Fire Club Caves, Raymond stopped and picked up Victor's Bowie knife. They walked slowly to the Bentley and once inside the luxurious car, Raymond didn't waste any time in putting the activities of the night far behind them. Soon they were crossing Exmoor. Then, at last, the Bentley turned into the driveway of The Five Pines, Joanna was asleep. Raymond parked the car and watched her for a moment. Then he whispered softly, 'Jo, we're home.'

He helped her out of the car and, taking his bag with the gun and Bowie knife still in it, they went inside .When they entered the lounge Rubin and Sam were waiting for them.

'It's good to see you both back safely!' said Rubin, 'although I'm afraid I have some bad news. Inspector Gibbins contacted me. He was looking for you but he said to inform you that Louis La Ronde and James Journal have escaped. Apparently, they managed to grab their weapons and ran deep into the caves. It wasn't safe to send his men after them. All the henchmen were arrested, mainly thanks to you, from what he said.'

'La Ronde tried to kill me,' said Joanna. 'He pointed his gun at me and pulled the trigger. This is going to sound crazy, but my guardian angel stepped in front of me and deflected the bullet. I could feel it through my crystal.' She ran a hand through her hair. 'I'm going to have to say goodnight, I think. I'm in desperate need of a shower and I need to wash the blood out of my hair.'

As soon as she left the room, Rubin asked, 'What was that about a guardian angel?'

'La Ronde fired at her at point blank range. Jo says the crystal around her neck started to vibrate, and brought forth a guardian angel,' he lowered his voice, 'but I saw a mark on one of the bars where the bullet ball ricocheted off and missed her. Her guardian angel was one of the steel bars. She's lucky to be alive and I don't want to place her in any more danger, ever again.'

'I am sorry to say it, Ray, but I don't think we have seen the last of Louis La Ronde and James Journal.'

'Uncle Rubin, I think you are right,' he answered. Then Raymond produced Victor's knife and placed it on the shelf just above the fire place.

'That's a nasty looking weapon,' remarked Sam. Raymond opened his bag and took out a towel. He unwrapped it to reveal another Bowie knife and a gun. 'I took these from La Ronde's men just before we left the Isles of Scilly.'

'Lock them away until you can give them to Inspector Gibbins, or someone like him,' suggested Rubin.

'That's a good idea,' said Sam.

15

The next few days passed peacefully, Joanna stayed at The Five Pines for a day or two, then returned to her own cottage. Sam explained that he had to go back to the test track and would leave that afternoon. Rubin thanked Sam for his help in dealing with Oliver, the henchman with the bald head. 'You should have seen him, Ray. Did you know that your friend can box? What was the combination, Sam! Three left jabs and a right cross?'

'That's right, that is what I usually use, not that I make a habit of it,' replied Sam with a big smile. Raymond could see that Rubin had enjoyed the spectacle. Rubin also enjoyed Raymond's company very much and he had not said anything about returning to his own house in York.

Then, in the early afternoon, the telephone rang and Raymond engaged in a lengthy conversation. When he returned to the lounge Sam was saying goodbye to Rubin.

'Thanks for the holiday, Ray,'

'I wouldn't say boxing with Oliver was much of a holiday.'

'Any time away from work is a holiday,' smiled Sam. 'Come and visit the test track any time.'

'Thanks, Sam. I will.'

Then he turned to Rubin. 'The phone call was my cousin Richard. He is in London with your brother and Francesca. He wanted to know if I would collect them. They would like to stay for a few days.'

'Oh, that would be wonderful! I haven't seen Michael in years.' Raymond could see that Rubin was genuinely pleased.

'I'll take the Bentley; and we'll see you in a few hours. Come on, Sam, I will take you home.' They left Rubin taking a seat in the bay window. He watched the Bentley move along the drive and leave the grounds. Then he went in search of one of his Havana cigars.

After Raymond had taken Sam home, his original plan had been to go to the airport to collect his cousin and two friends, but he decided to visit Louis La Ronde's Second-Hand Antique Shop first. This was really just out of curiosity, and to make sure that Mr. Sommers and Francesca would be safe. He was not expecting any trouble when he arrived, and he hoped that his adversary had really gone, so he parked the Bentley directly outside.

When he tried the door, it was locked, so after making sure he wasn't being watched, he gave the door a vicious kick just under the lock and it flew open. He entered, closing the door behind him. The shop was completely empty. He pushed past the curtains at the back of the shop and ventured into the dark passage. The last time he was here he had a man with a gun behind him. He climbed the darkened stairway and once at the top, pushed the door open.

The whole place had been cleaned out, not an antique anywhere. Even the swimming pool had been drained. Raymond couldn't decide if this was a good sign or not. But he didn't have the time to look through the place thoroughly, so he contented himself with the thought that the dealings with Louis La Ronde were finished.

He left the shop knowing that La Ronde's headquarters were no more. He had decided not to pursue him; it was up to the police to find him now. As he continued his journey, another thought crossed his mind. He said out loud, 'What about Francesca and Jo, they are almost certain to talk to each other, and while I do like Fran very much, I love Jo.' With his mind clear regarding the feelings he had for the girls, he parked the Bentley and went to find his friends.

The journey back to The Five Pines was quiet, Richard sat in the front and talked about being glad to come back to England. Mr. Sommers and his daughter sat in the back and didn't say much about anything, which seemed out of character for them both.

Eventually the Bentley turned off the main road and wound its way through the grounds. As it entered the turning circle, Raymond noticed that Joanna's Alfa Romeo was parked next to his Ferrari. He parked the Bentley, then opened and held the rear door for his friends. Richard proceeded to open and take two cases out of the boot. Then Raymond led them into the house.

Rubin had lit the log fire in the lounge and was waiting for them. As they entered, he rose to his feet and hugged his brother. 'Michael! It's so good to see you again.'

'It's good to see you too,' Mr. Sommers replied with a big smile. While the two older men talked, so did the two sisters. Francesca had told Joanna about their Austrian trip, about how she had met Raymond and the events involving Louis La Ronde. Joanna told her sister what she knew of Louis La Ronde and the journey to the Isles of Scilly, including their adventure regarding Captain Journal. She also told her of the moonlit night on the beach and the wish Raymond made on a shooting star.

Raymond took this opportunity to get to know Richard better. He was just a little taller than Raymond, and a bit rounder in the stomach area. Richard wanted to know about Louis La Ronde and how he could help to end the problem. Raymond explained the situation to the point where he had visited La Ronde's shop earlier that morning, and how he thought the danger may have passed now.

The two girls made coffee and sandwiches for everyone and by the end of the afternoon it had been agreed that they would all stay at The Five Pines, at least for the moment.

When the two girls, Rubin and Michael had retired for the night, Richard was able to go into detail about what had happened in Switzerland. He spoke in almost a whisper.

'I was only looking after Fran and her father, as you asked me too. We did all the tourist things in the first week or so and then Michael, Fran's father, started finding things to do, not to come with us. I was concerned at first but then it became apparent that he wanted us to spend more time together. I asked him for Fran's hand. He was happy that I asked and advised me to ask Fran when we were back in Britain. This is partly why we all came home.' Richard lowered his voice to a whisper. 'I am going to ask Fran to marry me, soon.'

Raymond grabbed Richard's hand and began to shake it.

'Congratulations!' he said warmly.

'Not so loud. I haven't asked her yet.'

'If she is like her sister Jo, she already knows.'

'Do you think so?'

'Don't waste any time, ask her,' Raymond said with enthusiasm. Then Richard changed the subject and asked, 'Is the Louis La Ronde thing really over?'

'His henchmen are in custody, but unfortunately he, and a dangerous man named Captain James Journal, are still at large.'

'Are they any threat to you?'

'They could be, but I'll deal with that when and if it happens. We must look to the future. Have you a plan in mind.'

'I thought I might look for a job here.'

'That sounds like a good plan, of course you can stay with me for as long as you like. Get used to the place, get to know some people.'

'Thanks, Ray,' he paused. 'But now I need to get some rest. It's been a long day.'

'If you are sure I can't offer you a brandy night cap?'

'Thank you, Ray, but I'll see you in the morning.'

'Good night, Richard,' He left the lounge and Raymond was alone. As the night grew into the early hours of the morning, he picked up Victor's knife from the shelf above the fire place, and sat down on the settee just aimlessly staring at it. His attention was drawn from the knife when Joanna entered the room and sat close to him on the settee.

'It's a horrible thing,' she said, 'why would anyone want a knife like that?'

'If you have time, I can tell you the answer to your question.'

'Is it a bedtime story?' she asked.

'Not what you would call a bedtime story, but if you like stories and legends of the old American West you may like this fantastic story.'

'I do like American history, like General Custer's last stand. I know that didn't turn out too well, but there were lots of stories that did, like Buffalo Bill, and Annie Oakley.'

She leaned against him and he placed the knife on his knee. 'This story is a bit like Custer's last stand in as much as there were no survivors. It was spring in the year of 1836 and, facing incredible odds, fewer than 200 men of all races defended a small Texas fort for 13 days against an army of soldiers led by the dictator of Mexico, General Santa Anna. The man in command was Colonel Travers, and the other two men that gave the small band of men the courage to stop Santa Anna, were Davy Crockett and Jim Bowie.'

'I've read about Davy Crockett,' remarked Joanna.

'The story of the Bowie knife began some years before. It is said, and this is only a legend, that Jim Bowie had made camp for the night and while lying on his bedroll looking up at the stars, he, perchance, saw a meteor streaking across the dark sky, and it landed not far away. At daybreak he went in search of the meteorite and found it.'

'That would be like a shooting star,' interrupted Joanna.

'It appeared to be a pool of metal, so he dug it out of the ground and took it home with him. He took it to a blacksmith, a James Black who told him he had never seen anything like it before. So Jim Bowie asked him if he could forge it into a knife. He drew a design and left it with him. Within a few days, James Black had made the first Bowie knife. He gave it to Jim Bowie, saying that the design of the knife would make it very desirable for woodsmen and frontier men, of which there were many. But, because of the composition of the metal used in making this knife, the first knife, there would only ever be the one Bowie knife. Jim Bowie travelled the West and was the guest of many Indian tribes. While he stayed with them, he showed them how to make hunting knives using his knife as a template. This is how the Bowie knife became so famous. There is the famous 'sand bar knife fight' that took place while Jim Bowie was acting as a second at a duel. The whole thing got out of hand and Bowie killed three men with his knife. Then he went on to fight at the Alamo.

'What happened to it, the real knife?' Joanna asked with interest.

'It was never found after the battle of the Alamo, only the many copies that were made exist, making it the most famous knife in the West. This one, Victor's knife, is a modern copy of the real thing. Even in Britain, Sheffield Steel makes and exports Bowie knives to America. Would you say it was a wish that came true?'

'It would seem to me that if a shooting star could grant wishes, that one did,' answered Joanna.

'What about our shooting star? The one we saw on the sub-tropical island of Tresco,' asked Raymond.

Joanna rested her head on Raymond's shoulder, 'I think it should grant us your wish,' she whispered. Raymond took the opportunity that he hadn't expected.

'Jo, will you marry me?'

She raised her head from his shoulder and looked into his eyes. 'You're sure of what you are wishing for?'

'I have loved you from the moment...'

She put her fingers gently over his lips.

'I have loved you since I saw you getting out of your Bentley and sending Victor and Oliver back to their boss empty handed. Yes, Ray, I will marry you,' she paused. 'Would you say our shooting star has granted our wish?'

'Yes,' he answered. Joanna rested her head back on Raymond's shoulder and closed her eyes. She felt warm, she felt safe, she felt wanted and loved, and soon she was asleep. Raymond watched the logs in the fire place, as they radiated a warming red glow. He took the Bowie knife from his knee and let it drop onto the carpet, in just a few minutes he closed his eyes and fell asleep too.

The following morning when Raymond opened his eyes, the fire had burned itself out, and Joanna was still asleep, her head on his shoulder. He moved her gently placing her head on a soft cushion. As he rose silently from the settee, he retrieved the Bowie knife and placed it on the shelf above the fire place, then went in search of coffee. When he returned, he had a mug in each hand and Joanna was awake. He offered one of the mugs to her. 'Coffee?' he said. She reached out and took it.

'Ray,' she said, 'will you come with me, back to my cottage? I've made something for you, and I'd like to give it to you, now.' They finished their coffee; and Raymond picked up the Bowie knife from the shelf as they left. They took Joanna's car. Rubin was awake and just missed them, but he watched the Alfa Romeo leave the grounds from the bay window. As he turned from the window, his brother Michael entered.

'You've just missed Ray, and Jo; they've taken the Alfa Romeo somewhere.'

'They're two good kids. Did they have any breakfast?' Michael asked.

'Only coffee, I think.'

'Must be something very important to take them out so early.'

'I think love is in the air,' remarked Rubin.

'How did you know that? It was supposed to be a secret,' said Michael.

'What was supposed to be a secret?' asked his brother.

'Richard and Fran, this is one of the reasons that they came back from Switzerland. They are going to be married.'

'That's good news, she couldn't find a nicer man,' said Rubin. Then his brother said, 'When you said love is in the air, you weren't talking about Richard and Fran, where you?'

'No, I didn't know about Richard and Fran, I was talking about Ray and Jo. They haven't said anything about marriage, but I am sure Jo would say yes if he asked her.'

Then Michael changed the subject, 'I do hope that we have seen the last of Louis La Ronde.'

'I hope so too,' agreed Rubin, he gave a worried sigh and said. 'But, with La Ronde and Captain Journal still at large, we may not be free of them.' There was silence between the two brothers for a moment. Then the two men left the lounge and went in search of some coffee.

16

It was mid-morning when the Alfa Romeo arrived outside Joanna's cottage; she switched off the engine and jumped over the driver's door.

'We need to go down into my workshop,' she said as she unlocked and pushed open the front door. Raymond followed her, taking the knife with him. She opened the trapdoor and they made their way down the wooden staircase to the lapidary workshop. Joanna felt for the switch and put the lights on. Though Raymond had been there before he hadn't realised how big the workshop was. He looked around and, situated in the middle of the workbench, was a snow globe. Joanna picked it up and with a flick of her wrist she sent all the tiny sparkling particles flying around inside it. She gave it to Raymond.

'This is for you,' she said with a smile, her blue eyes shining like the particles inside the glass globe.

'The crystal in the centre is the copy I made of the Snowflake Diamond.' Raymond looked at it closely, 'What are the sparkling bits made of?' he asked.

'They are tiny diamond chips; I made it so that it would look like…'

Raymond interrupted her, 'Like a mountain.'

'Yes, I even put a label on the base,' she took the glass globe from him and turned it around. 'See?' she said.

'It's beautiful, Jo,' he said, as he read the label, 'The Crystal Mountain'. She gave it back to him. He flicked his wrist and the diamond chips sparkled as they glided around the crystal.

'What fluid did you use to make the chips float down so slowly?'

'I can't tell you all my secrets,' she looked at him, 'and I can't keep anything from you,' She reached out and kissed him. 'It's thin, transparent oil.' She moved away from him and Raymond placed the knife on the workbench. 'It could be part of your American Indian collection; it wouldn't look out of place next to the dream catcher.'

'Thank you, Ray. I will find a place for it.' Then she reached out and took Raymond's hand, 'Did you mean what you said last night, about our wish on the shooting star?'

'Yes, I did.' He looked into her blue eyes, 'I do love you,' he whispered, 'We could go back to The Five Pines and tell everyone that we want to get married.'

'Not yet,' answered Joanna. She continued, 'Last night, Fran told me that Richard had asked her to marry him while they were in Switzerland. They came home so that we could all be together for their happy day. Let's wait to share our news, at least for a while.'

'If that is what you want, we can wait.' Joanna sensed his disappointment even though Raymond didn't say anything. Then she said, 'My father had known about Richard and Fran before they came home. He has been keeping the secret, so would you mind if we tell Rubin? Then he can keep a secret, too.' She smiled and her blue eyes sparkled. 'That's a good idea,' he said, then added, 'but only Uncle Rubin.'

Joanna broke the atmosphere of the moment, 'Let's go back and tell Uncle Rubin right now.' Raymond picked up the snow globe and they left the lapidary.

Joanna was so happy, he could tell, in the warm

sunshine and, with the breeze blowing her golden hair, as she put the Alfa Romeo through its paces. He enjoyed being driven and she was very good at it. The journey was all too short for him and it wasn't long before the Alfa Romeo entered the grounds of Raymond's house.

They found everyone in the lounge as usual. Joanna said to Francesca, 'Come with me,' she took her sister's hand, 'I think the men have some things to arrange.' They both left the room and went in search of something for lunch.

Raymond placed the snow globe on the shelf above the fire place; he moved it once or twice and then he said, 'Gentlemen, it seems we have some things to arrange.'

Raymond and Richard sat on the settee, while Michael and Rubin sat at the table near the bay window. They were all silent until Michael, not being able to keep the secret any longer said, 'It's about a wedding, isn't it?' He went on, 'Sorry, Richard, but I told Rubin this morning.'

'Then our secret is out,' said Richard.

'Sorry Richard, Jo told me this morning, too,' added Raymond.

'I may be old fashioned, but I would still like you to ask the question,' said Michael.

'What question?' asked Richard.

'THE question,' Raymond said. 'Come on, Richard, you know what to ask the father of the bride,' urged Raymond, then he whispered, 'Please may I have your daughter's hand…'

'Oh, but we arranged all that before we left Switzerland.'

'Well, say it again,' whispered Raymond. Richard

rose from the settee and stood in front of Mr. Sommers. 'Sir, please may I...' Just then the door opened and Joanna and Francesca entered the lounge with a tray of sandwiches and tea which they put on the table.

Richard cleared his throat, 'Sir, please may I have Francesca's hand in marriage?'

'Of course, you can, my boy,' came the welcome answer, 'I know you will look after her.'

'Thank you, sir,' Richard said with relief. Francesca was unable to contain her happiness and put her arms around her father. 'Can we start to arrange the wedding?' she asked enthusiastically.

'Yes, certainly you can. Let me know when you want some money!'

They all enjoyed lunch, the mood was jubilant with the happy couple and a very pleased father and uncle. While they were so happy, Raymond said to his cousin, 'Richard, you'll be looking for some work?'

'Yes, I will.'

'I can introduce you to a friend who has a vacancy.'

'A vacancy for what?'

'Why don't you come with me and see if you will like the job?'

'That would be most welcome. When will you be able to arrange a meeting?'

'What about now?' Richard rose to his feet and Raymond joined him.

'Would you all please excuse us?' Raymond asked, 'We have to go and see a man about a car.' They left the lounge, Raymond leading the way.

Once outside, Raymond said, 'Let's take the Ferrari.' He threw the keys into the air, Richard caught them. They opened the doors and slid into the low-slung sports car. Richard turned the key and the engine burst into life. As they drove, the two men talked about marriage and how it could change their lives. They both agreed it was time to settle down and that Richard couldn't have chosen a better girl to spend his life with. Neither of them had known Francesca or Joanna long, but Richard just knew it was right, and although Raymond didn't say anything about Joanna, he knew it was right too.

Richard increased the speed, 'It's very lively, isn't it?'

'There's a long straight piece of road around that next bend, if it's safe, open her up a bit.' As they came out of the curve, the road ahead was clear. Richard changed down a gear and pushed his foot to the floor. The car increased in speed and they were pushed back into their seats, Richard changed gear again and the Ferrari was rapidly approaching its top speed.

'You could have held that last gear a fraction longer.'

'I didn't like to, it's not my car,' replied Richard.

'Better slow down, at least to the speed limit,' said Raymond, 'we need to take the next road on the left.' The turning came into sight and they approached it quickly, Richard applied the brakes and changed down the gears, he turned the car off the main road and stopped in a car park.

'What was all that about?' he asked, as he switched off the engine. 'I felt like I was taking my driving test again.'

'You'll see. We have to walk from here.' They walked a short distance and then entered a small building. Richard found himself in an office. Sitting behind a desk was a big, black man dressed in what looked like racing overalls. He looked up and a smile flooded over his face, 'Ray! Good to see you, what brings you here?'

'Sam, I would like to introduce you to my cousin, Richard. He's looking for a job.'

'Can he do what you used to do?'

'Why don't we find out? Do you have a car that needs a test drive?'

'It just so happens that I do.'

'Not to destruction,' said Raymond hopefully.

'You'll find some fireproof overalls in there,' Sam was pointing at a changing room. Richard went in and very soon he reappeared looking quite different in a pair of racing overalls.

Sam handed Richard a crash helmet, 'Come with me,' he said. The three men left the office and walked to the test track. There, waiting to be tested, was a prototype sports car.

'Richard, will you take it for a few laps, then park it and tell me what you've found.'

'I am not a mechanic, I have an interest in cars as a hobby, but I am no expert.' Richard put the crash helmet on and fitted himself into the driver's seat; he pulled the seat belts around him as tight as he could, and locked the buckle. The radio in his crash helmet spoke to him, 'When you are ready, start the engine. You're good to go.'

Richard started the engine and the prototype moved away very smoothly. Richard gave it two laps to get used to the car and to familiarise himself with the track. The voice in his crash helmet gave him another instruction, 'Richard, increase the speed as much as you feel safe.' As the car passed for the third time, Sam started his stopwatch. Richard passed them twice at racing speed, then the radio delivered some more instructions, 'That will be all thanks, Richard, bring it in and park it at the end of this lap.' Richard carried out the last instruction and parked the prototype where he had found it. He hit the release button of his safety harness and opened the door. Richard climbed out of the car slowly. Removing his crash helmet revealed a huge grin on his face. But before he had time to say anything, Sam asked, 'What are your findings?'

'It'll make a very impressive sports car, but there is the smallest hint of a misfire on the top end of the speed range in all the gears. I suspect engine electrics, and there is something not quite right with the top gear in the final drive. It's as if it was trying to catch up with itself.'

Sam reached out and grabbed Richard by the shoulders as though he was a long lost relative. 'I tested this car this morning and these were my findings exactly. Was there anything else?'

Richard thought for a moment, 'Oil pressure, yes. It was low for the first two laps, but then it increased and so it wasn't necessary to stop the test.'

'There's a job here for you if you want it. You don't have to be a mechanic, you just need to feel what the car is telling you.'

'Thanks!' replied Richard with a smile.

'Not all the tests are like this, sometimes it can get dangerous. Come back to the office and I'll explain in detail.'

'Sam, is there a company car?' asked Raymond.

'For Richard, of course there is.'

'I'll leave you to sort out the details then. Thanks,

Sam.' He shook hands with his old friend and walked back to his Ferrari. Driving home, he felt satisfied with the day's achievements.

When he arrived back at The Five Pines, it was late afternoon. On entering the lounge, he found Joanna and Francesca sitting at the table, perusing their planning notes for the wedding. Michael and Rubin were sitting on the settee.

'Can I help?' he said cheerfully.

'No thanks,' was the reply from the table. But there was a different answer from the settee.

It was Michael, 'I think we need to talk to you, my boy.' Raymond sat between the two brothers.

'How can I help you?' he asked.

Michael began to explain, 'We need to plan living arrangements for after the wedding, Jo and you would stay here at The Five Pines.'

'But we are not married,' Raymond said in a quiet voice.

'But you will be, won't you? Sorry, Ray, I was never any good at keeping secrets,' said Rubin. 'I told Michael about you and Jo when we started to plan where and how to find a place for all of us. It made everything so much easier knowing that you and Jo would live here. I am going to sell the house in York and move in with Michael, the cottage will be perfect for us to live out our retirement. There will be enough money for us to live comfortably.'

'What about Francesca and Richard?' asked Raymond.

'We were hoping that they could move into Jo's cottage. Actually, it's my cottage and I was going to give it to Richard and Fran as a wedding present,' stated Rubin.

'What about her lapidary. She would be lost without it.'

'We could have it moved here. There must be a room in this big house for Jo's crystals,' suggested Michael.

'Of course, there's plenty of room. I'm all for it, if the girls agree, but Jo and I hadn't planned to get married yet. We would like Fran and Richard to have their happy day and then we will set a date.'

'You won't forget to ask the question, will you, my boy?' smiled Michael.

'When the time comes, I will,' he answered.

'Then that's settled,' said Rubin, 'I shall talk to some people, solicitor, estate agents, Vicar and I won't forget the bank.'

Raymond rose from the settee and crossed the room to the table. He leaned over and put his arms around Jo, 'Uncle Rubin has spread are news,' he said.

'Congratulations,' Francesca said, as she looked up at him, 'I am really happy for both of you,' she smiled.

'I am glad that you and Richard found each other too,' he said. She held out her hand and he took it. Then he looked at Joanna, 'Is everything going to plan?' he asked.

'Yes, everything,' answered Joanna, beaming up at him.

* * *

The weeks had passed and all was going smoothly. A date was set for the wedding and work was carried out to move Joanna's lapidary into one of the bigger rooms in The Five Pines.

Richard had settled into working with Sam and

the safety team. He had worked to the instructions of at least two red files. Sam and the team had been there for him and a bond was fast forming between them.

There were just a few days left before the wedding day; dresses had been fitted, invitations had been sent, floral arrangements had been made. Raymond and Richard had been told that they had to move out of The Five Pines before the wedding day and so they were living in Michael's cottage.

Richard had extended an invitation to Sam, who by now was a good friend of Richard's as well as an old friend of Raymond's. He had been delighted with the invitation so Richard also extended it to include the safety team.

17

Raymond's Ferrari and Richard's company car, a Porsche, were parked in the driveway of the cottage. Their suits for the wedding had arrived that morning and they were trying them on to make sure they looked immaculate for the big day. They had decided to dress the same; a long black coat with matching trousers, a silver waistcoat with a white shirt and a black and silver cravat with a diamond pin. When they looked at each other, it was like looking into a mirror.

'Which one of us is getting married?' asked Richard jovially.

'Hard to tell the difference,' replied Raymond. 'We both look the part.'

'You might be a look-alike, but I am marrying Francesca.'

'You look good,' remarked Raymond.

'And for a best man, so do you,' said his cousin.

The wedding would be in just a few days and The Five Pines was a hive of activity. There were cars coming and going constantly, with caterers, hair stylists and manicurists, even the Vicar came just to make sure all the details he had were correct.

In the evenings, when Richard was on his way home from the test track, he would drive past The Five Pines, just to see all the effort that was being put into the wedding. He had done this a few times, but had never gone in, or made his presence known. But twice he had noticed a black Mercedes parked off the main road and just clear of the driveway to The Five Pines.

Richard mentioned the black Mercedes to

Raymond. He was concerned, for Raymond had encountered a black Mercedes before, and the men driving it had tried to kidnap Joanna. The day before the wedding, the cousins took the Porsche back to The Five Pines and waited. About mid-afternoon the black Mercedes showed up. From what they could see, there were two men in it. They had concealed the car well, but they only sat there and watched.

'What do you think they want?' asked Richard.

'If they've been doing this for a few days, I suspect they are, as they say, casing the joint. We need to find out who they are.' Then the black car moved from its cover and raced away.

'They've spotted us! Follow it, Richard!'

Richard started the Porsche and went in pursuit of the Mercedes. The speed increased and soon they had left Exmoor and found themselves on the motorway, heading for London. Their target had no respect for speed limits; Richard had to take the Porsche to 115 miles an hour just to keep the Mercedes in sight.

As they entered the outskirts of London, the speed was reduced and, after the motorway, the streets of London were much slower. Raymond soon recognised the area. It was no surprise that the Mercedes stopped outside Louis La Ronde's Second-Hand Antique Shop. Richard drove passed and then parked the powerful car.

'Who would have thought to look for La Ronde at his old headquarters?' remarked Richard.

'Foolhardy, or a clever double bluff, depending on your point of view,' said Raymond, 'let's find out what they want.'

The two men left the Porsche and approached the

shop on foot. Raymond tried the door. It was unlocked so they entered cautiously. The shop wasn't full of antiques, but it housed most of what Raymond had seen at the Hell-Fire Club Caves. There was a lot of military memorabilia, a few British and German helmets, an array of bayonets, four second world war hand grenades and a glass case full of medals, German, British and American. They slipped silently through the shop and opened the curtains at the back. Richard followed Raymond through the dark passage and up the stairs. Now they were at the door to Louis La Ronde's office-come-penthouse.

Slowly, Raymond pushed it open and there, sitting at his desk in all his finery of lace and silks, was Louis La Ronde. They entered. Raymond approached La Ronde slowly, not taking his eyes off him. Then the door slammed shut behind them. They spun round and there was Captain James Journal, standing behind the door, pointing a gun at them. They had fallen for the oldest trick in the book. La Ronde smiled and removed the flintlock pistol from one of the desk drawers and pointed it at them.

'The police have already been here searching for me. I didn't think anyone would come back. The best place to hide is where they've already looked, don't you think?' Then he asked, 'And who's your friend?'

'I'm Ray's cousin,' replied Richard.

'Were you the men in the Mercedes who have been watching my house? I know you're involved, they led us straight to your shop.'

'You didn't recognise me? I think I might be insulted, Mr. Spade.'

'Surprise me, La Ronde. Why were you there?'

'You stopped me delivering the Snowflake

Diamond, the only time I have ever failed and, as a consequence I have been asked for your life. I have a reputation to uphold.' La Ronde stood up. 'I am the second-hand man, I can obtain anything for anyone. I have only ever failed one client and that is the man pointing a gun at you.' He paused. 'I hear you're getting married tomorrow.'

'I am,' answered Richard.

'No. You're not. I'm going to make sure you are both here with me, or better yet dead. One way or another I will see you never make it to that church.'

This enraged Raymond. He jumped onto the desk, kicking the pistol out of La Ronde's hand. When Richard realised what Raymond was doing, he spun around, pushing away the gun that Captain Journal was holding, and landing a substantial punch into his stomach. Everything happened so fast. Captain Journal was stumbling backwards and, as he did, he grabbed the back of a wooden chair and hurled it at Richard. One of the wooden legs caught him on his right cheekbone. He fell backwards and found himself, dazed, sitting on the floor.

Raymond wasn't fairing much better for, as the pistol was kicked out of La Ronde's hand, his other hand grabbed an ornate walking stick from the desk. He hit Raymond at the back of his knees and, as he fell, he hit the corner of the desk with his left eyebrow. Everything went white for a moment and, when he opened his eyes, he was on the floor with two men trying to pull him to his feet.

'I know both of you, don't I? The last time I saw you, we were diving on the Association. You should be locked up on Saint Mary's.'

'Not enough proof,' answered one of the men.

'You and the Captain had gone when the police chopper picked us up. We thanked them for saving us from drowning, so it was difficult to charge us with anything when you and our boat had disappeared.' Then he added, 'You left us to drown.'

'It was no more than you were trying to do to me,' retorted Raymond.

'You know these two?' asked Richard with surprise.

'We're acquainted,' Raymond answered. 'La Ronde,' he said, 'at least I have the satisfaction of knowing Victor, Oliver and Ginger are in police custody.'

La Ronde had retrieved his gun and now took its twin from a jewelled, wooden box. He pointed both guns at Raymond and Richard.

'There was a bit of a mishap at the hospital, Ginger caused such a fuss that it created a perfect diversion for Victor and Oliver. They became separated from him. When they had been treated, they just walked out of the hospital.'

'Both you and Journal managed to evade the police at the Hell-Fire Club Caves. Just how did you do that?'

'There are escape passages that aren't in the guide book. Remember, the people who used the club, like Sir Francis Dashwood, Lord Sandwich, Lord of the Admiralty, peers of the realm like that, could not allow themselves to be caught! So, you see, we're in good company!'

'That is unfortunate,' said Raymond.

'Alright, enough of how things were done. Just stand still. If either of you moves, I will shoot you both,' threatened La Ronde.

'I would like to know how you robbed the security van?' remarked Raymond.

'That, you will never know, I will take that secret to my grave.'

'Would I be right in thinking hypnosis was used at some point, because it was effective at Rubin's house.'

'Get them out of London and shoot them!' ordered Captain Journal impatiently.

'Alright!' answered La Ronde. 'You two men, lead the way. James, you walk behind them with me. Spade, don't try anything, I can't miss at this distance.'

'If you do, I won't,' Captain Journal added.

They left the office-come-penthouse and stepped carefully down the stairs, slowly making their way through the dark passage and entering the shop floor. The two big men walked to the door and opened it, but Raymond had slowed his pace while passing the military memorabilia. Suddenly, he reached out and snatched a hand grenade from the display. He spun around so that he was face to face with Louis La Ronde.

'Spade!' he shouted, clearly alarmed. Raymond looked him in the eyes and pulled the pin out of the grenade.

'Don't be a fool, you'll kill us all,' Captain Journal said with a sense of urgency. When the two henchmen realised what was happening behind them, they made a run for the door and escaped out of the shop.

'Your backup seems to have deserted you,' Raymond said with a smile.

'Put the pin back in the grenade!' ordered Captain Journal.

'That grenade is eighty years old. What makes

you think it's live?' bluffed La Ronde.

'The fact that you looked and sounded very concerned when I pulled the pin tells me that you don't know if it's live or not and, from the expression on your face, I would say it's live.'

Richard and Raymond backed slowly away from Journal and La Ronde, not taking their eyes off them for a second. When they reached the open door, to their dismay, their path was blocked by the two men waiting outside. One of them started to take something out of his pocket. Richard grabbed his hand and wrestled the gun from him, tearing his coat as he did.

'I trust it's loaded,' he said, as he pointed it at them. La Ronde and Journal started to approach them slowly.

'Put the gun down,' said La Ronde.

'Oh no, I can't do that. You might try to shoot me,' Richard said as he turned to face them, at the same time keeping an eye on the two men. Then Raymond asked, 'Why are you still carrying those antiques? They're notoriously inaccurate.'

'He's right,' agreed Captain Journal. 'That's why you missed that Sommers girl in the caves.'

'If you had killed her, you wouldn't be standing here now,' said Raymond.

'You wouldn't stoop so low as to commit murder, would you, Mr. Spade?'

'You don't know me, La Ronde.' Raymond indicated to the two big men to move away from the door. They obeyed, as he was still holding the hand grenade.

'Come on, Richard, it's time to leave.'

Richard stepped past his cousin, taking care not

to push him because he didn't want Raymond to drop the grenade either.

'Stay away from us, La Ronde, I have told you once before what will happen if you harm me or mine, and that goes for you too, Journal.'

'I have a contract, Spade, and I will carry it out,'

Raymond and Richard left the Second-Hand Antique Shop, and when they were sure they were not being followed Raymond replaced the pin into the hand grenade. They hastened back to where they had parked the Porsche and, once inside the car, Richard drove at some speed out of London.

'You look worried,' he said.

'La Ronde wasn't watching The Five Pines for nothing. He may try something there or at the church. When we get back I'll call Inspector Gibbins and tell him La Ronde has returned to his shop, I might even invite him to the wedding.'

The journey from London passed quickly, though it was about two in the morning when they reached the cottage on Exmoor. They cleaned themselves up and tried to get a few hours' sleep before the wedding day.

It was passed eight o'clock when Raymond awoke. Seeing the time he hastily went to wake his cousin. While Richard was getting into his wedding suit, Raymond contacted Inspector Gibbins. Raymond was lucky and was not held up by the sergeant on the desk, who put him through to the Inspector immediately. As Richard was passing, he overheard Raymond say, 'It'll be good to see you again. The wedding is at twelve noon in the little church just outside Porlock.' Then there was silence as Raymond listened to Inspector Gibbins. 'If you can't make it, come to The Five Pines for the reception'. He replaced the receiver and went to find Richard.

'He said he may not get to the church on time, but he will come to the reception. He also confirmed what La Ronde said about Victor and Oliver. They did escape from the hospital.'

'Then we haven't seen the last of them,' concluded Richard.

'Come on Richard, I'd like to take the Ferrari back to The Five Pines and we can go on from there in the Bentley.'

They had to remove their top hats to fit themselves into the Ferrari. It wasn't a long drive back to The Five Pines. When they arrived, the driveway and turning circle were busy with people getting the house ready for the reception. There was a Rolls Royce and a Bentley parked directly outside the front door and two vans with catering staff going in and out of the house carrying all kinds of nice things to eat.

Raymond parked the Ferrari next to the Alfa Romeo, and they both slipped, unseen, into the Bentley. Raymond started the engine and drove it from the turning circle, parking it between the trees just off the driveway.

'I was going to ask Sam to follow the wedding cars in case there was any trouble from La Ronde and Journal but, with our trip to London last night, I haven't spoken to him. It looks like we will have to protect them from any attack ourselves.'

'We'll have to hope they don't go for a road block,' remarked Richard.

'I think that might be more difficult to achieve. They would have to interfere with more traffic and more people to do that,' concluded Raymond.

They didn't have to wait long for Francesca and Joanna to came out of the house with Rubin and their father. They were helped into the wedding cars by the two chauffeurs.

Raymond and Richard waited patiently until the wedding cars had passed. Then they left the grounds of The Five Pines and followed the Rolls Royce and the Bentley at a discreet distance.

'We have to stay behind them,' stated Raymond.

'We're the ones that supposed to be waiting for them at the church,' remarked Richard. 'They're the ones who are supposed to be late!'

'We need to make sure that they get there,' said Raymond.

They had only travelled a few miles when Raymond observed a black Mercedes in the rear-view mirror steadily gaining on them. It came closer and closer until Raymond could see the men in the car.

'We have company. La Ronde's henchmen. Last time I met them I put them both in hospital.'

The Mercedes began to move from behind the Bentley and came alongside it. Raymond was right; the two men in it were Victor and Oliver. Oliver was driving. He allowed the Mercedes to drop back into Raymond's blind spot, so that he couldn't see it in his mirrors. Raymond might not have been able to see the Mercedes, but he just knew they were going to try to run him off the road.

He had already seen the result when he first met Joanna. He remembered the black paint on the front of her Alfa Romeo. The Mercedes drew alongside the Bentley and lingered for a second or two. Then Raymond sensed the gap between the two cars closing. Suddenly, he stepped hard on the brakes. The seat belts locked and the car went down hard on the front suspension. The front wheels locked and smoke poured from the tyres as the Mercedes swept across the front of the Bentley, hitting the front wing and smashing the driver's side headlight. The Mercedes met little or no resistance as it continued its journey of destruction, crossing the path of the Bentley, going over the grass verge, making a large gap in the hedge and coming to rest in a field. Fortunately for Oliver and Victor, it was still on its wheels.

'That was close,' remarked Richard.

'Yes,' agreed Raymond, 'and you can bet they will try again if they get the chance.' Raymond increased the speed of the Bentley until the wedding cars were in site again. 'We will have to stay here and hope that there is another way into the church. It's the bride's prerogative to be late.'

'I don't want to start married life with excuses for being late for my own wedding, although being almost run of the road would be a good one.'

'If La Ronde's men can get their car out of the field, I would prefer to be between them and the wedding cars.'

They continued following the Rolls Royce and the Bentley. Raymond, in his own Bentley, was watching his mirrors for any sign of the black Mercedes, but there was none.

The two bridal cars at last stopped next to a quaint little church just outside Porlock. Raymond parked the Bentley and, trying not to be seen, they jumped over the church wall and walked through the graveyard. They made their way to the side of the church and entered through a small door that opened into the vestry. They walked straight into the choir, getting ready for the ceremony. Apologising profusely to the choir master and the choirboys, they turned to move on and Richard almost walked into the Vicar. It seemed to be instinctive as they both apologised together. The Vicar was rather portly with a balding head. He was dressed traditionally in a black cassock and white surplice with a round, white collar. His face just beamed with kindness.

'I know most of the young men I see before their weddings are nervous, but you know you could have come in through the main entrance.'

Then they heard the church organ start to play, 'Here Comes the Bride'. The Vicar hurried them out of the vestry and whispered to them, 'Take your places and, during the service, watch me. I will lead you. No matter what happens, when you leave this church, you'll be married.' The last remark was directed at Richard.

Richard and Raymond took their places and both could not resist looking to the back of the church to see the bride and her maid of honour walking down the aisle, accompanied by their father. When the organ stopped playing, Francesca and Joanna were standing beside them. The service started.

18

'Dearly beloved, we are gathered together here in the sight of God...'

As the service continued, the Vicar asked, 'If there is anyone amongst you that knows of any just cause or impediment why these two persons should not be joined together in holy matrimony, let them speak now, or forever hold their peace.' A silence filled the church, not a sound was heard. Then Raymond stepped forward with the gold ring. He gave it to the Vicar who in turn gave it to Richard. At the correct time he placed it on Francesca's finger. 'In the giving and receiving of this ring you declare your love for one another,' stated the Vicar, 'That which God has joined together, let no man put asunder. You may now kiss the bride!' Richard obeyed the instruction, and enjoyed it!

Richard and Francesca led the way down the aisle, followed by Raymond and Joanna. They, in turn, were followed by Michael and Rubin. Once outside, there were photographs to take in various beautiful situations around the church. Francesca asked her new husband, 'What happened to your eye? It's black.'

'I hit a chair with it,' answered Richard.

'And what happened to your eye?' asked Joanna.

'I hit a desk with it,' answered Raymond.

'The photographs should be alright. The photographer said he can touch them up a bit so the bruising won't show,' Richard said hopefully.

Raymond gave the keys for the Bentley to Michael and said, 'When the photographer is finished, would you and Uncle Rubin take the Bentley back to The Five Pines? Richard and I will follow in the wedding cars.'

After an hour of photographs, they at last left the beautiful little church, Richard and Francesca in the Rolls Royce and Raymond and Joanna in the Bentley. When they reached The Five Pines most of the guests were already there, including Inspector Gibbins. Raymond shook his hand, 'I am pleased that you could make it.'

'I wasn't in time for the ceremony, but I am here for the speeches and the meal.'

'Can you stay for the party this evening?'

'I wouldn't miss it. I have brought two plain clothes officers with me, just in case there is any trouble. I hope you don't mind.'

'Not at all, the more the merrier,' answered Raymond. He left the Inspector and, by the time he had greeted everyone, it was almost time for the wedding breakfast. Once everyone was seated, it was time for the speeches. This had been Richard's idea, he wanted the speeches first, before the meal, as he didn't want to suffer from nerves and not enjoy his meal. He had spoken to all who intended to speak and they agreed speeches first. Richard stood up and tapped a wine glass with a spoon. The room became very quiet.

'I have been practising tapping a wine glass for days to gain everyone's attention, fortunately I haven't broken this one.' The room remained quiet. 'If I had only remembered to wait for my best man to say, 'pray silence for the groom,' I wouldn't have practiced not breaking the wine glass at all.' The room still remained quiet. 'This wasn't how I intended to start my speech.' There was still no interaction with the guests. Then

Raymond, seeing his cousin was having a bit of trouble, stood up.

'Ladies and Gentlemen, pray silence for the groom, and don't forget the magic words.' A ripple of giggling filled the room.

'Ladies and Gentlemen, on behalf of my wife and I,' to which there was a round of applause and cheering, 'we would like to thank you all for being our guests on this happy day. But first I better explain about my black eye!' The speech was short but light-hearted. Raymond followed with a quick vote of thanks to everyone who attended, and then some witty remarks about Richard. He covered the black eye saying that it matched his suit and how difficult it was to punch each other in just the right place to obtain the matching affect that they had. This was met with another round of applause. When they had finished, the bride's father and uncle said a few words and then dinner was served. It all went perfectly. Everyone enjoyed their meal, right down to the last cup of coffee.

Then everyone moved to the next room where a band was playing and taking requests for music and songs from the guests. There were more drinks, sandwiches, cakes and trifle. The whole atmosphere was very jovial, with the band playing and all the guests laughing and talking. The Vicar had found Richard and explained that he had to leave. Richard tried to persuade him to stay, but he was adamant that he had to leave. He said his ears were very sensitive to the music, which was very tactful of him.

'I wish you and your lady wife well. God bless you both. Look after her.' They shook hands and Richard answered, 'I will, and thank you, Vicar.'

As the night wore on, one by one their guests started to leave. Raymond was relieved when the house fell silent. The last to leave were Sam and the safety team, but they could still be heard singing somewhere in the grounds of The Five Pines.

However, not all had left. There were three men remaining; Inspector Gibbins, and the two plain clothes officers.

'When you invited me to the wedding, I assumed you were expecting some kind of trouble, but everything seems to be under control. I would just like to say goodbye to both Mr. Sommers and the bride and groom before I leave.'

'I'll come with you; they should be in the lounge upstairs.' They climbed the carpeted stairs and walked along the landing.

'Have you ever considered becoming a private detective?' asked Inspector Gibbins.

'No, I haven't really thought about it,' replied Raymond.

'If you decide that one day you would like to make a difference, I will write a letter of introduction and give you some good references. I don't like private detectives, as a rule. They are always a bit hazy, you know, economical with the truth, but I think you and I could make a good team.'

'Thank you, Inspector, I will give it some thought.'

They reached the door to the lounge and pushed it open. When they entered, they didn't expect to see the scene that met their eyes.

Standing next to the fireplace in all his finery was Louis La Ronde and, sitting on the settee, were Michael and Rubin. Standing behind them was

Captain Journal and, near to the table by the bay window, were Victor and Oliver.

Raymond and Inspector Gibbins stepped into the lounge, Raymond closed the door.

'I don't remember inviting you to the reception,' he said.

'We invited ourselves,' answered Louis La Ronde. While your guests have been leaving through the front of the house, we entered through the back. I decided we would wait for you here. This is the room where you spend most of your time when you are at home, isn't it? I have visited you before and you showed me into this room when we had the conversation regarding Rubin.'

'Where are the other two? You know, Captain, your two divers.' Victor was the one who answered, 'They've gone back to the Isles of Scilly. Apparently they're not brave enough to take on a man with a hand grenade.'

Raymond picked up the hand grenade from the shelf over the fireplace and checked that the pin was secure, then replaced it.

'I don't know if it's live or not. La Ronde seemed to think it was when I used it to escape from him at our last meeting. I do know that there are at least three more like this one back at his shop.'

'I'll get some men to go through it and we'll make sure it won't be open for business,' Inspector Gibbins said casually.

Then La Ronde spoke. 'You haven't asked why I'm here. You know it isn't to wish the bride and groom a happy life together.'

'No, I wouldn't expect that.'

'Very good, Mr. Spade, but you can see I have

175

tried to dress to suit the occasion.'

'I think you are a trifle overdressed even for a wedding, but I must compliment you on your choice of attire, all your silks and laces, the waistcoat with the gold watch and chain, and I see you have two well-polished holsters, homes for your jewel encrusted flintlock pistols.'

Then La Ronde took one of the pistols from its holster and he pointed it at Raymond.

'I am the Second-Hand Man, but I haven't come to acquire an object this evening. I have come to complete a contract, on you, and Miss Sommers, a contract that my friend Captain Journal has already paid for. He is here to see it completed.'

Rubin was sitting close to his brother on the settee; he was concealing his sword stick between them. He wasn't going to sit still while his prospective son-in-law was shot and so, seizing the moment, he stood up and, as he did, Captain Journal moved from behind the settee and grabbed him. He took the sword stick away and drew the blade, pushing him back onto the settee saying, 'Sit down and don't move, you are just an old fool.'

'A little less of the old, if you don't mind,' Rubin said indignantly. Captain Journal drew back the blade, his intention to run Raymond through but, as he did, Raymond saw La Ronde's finger move on the trigger of the flintlock pistol. He saw the hammer fall and the flash in the pan. He moved sideways to avoid the sword and as he did, he felt something snatch at his coat. From behind him he heard Captain Journal cry out, 'Not me you idiot! Why must you use these damned antiques?!' He dropped the sword stick as he gripped his side. Rubin picked it up and held it ready.

Behind Raymond, Captain Journal fell to the floor and Inspector Gibbins went to his aid. Just then the lounge door opened and Joanna and Francesca entered the room. Victor and Oliver watched as La Ronde drew the second flintlock pistol from its holster and set the gun ready to be fired. Raymond knew he had no time to try anything so he dropped to one knee and a second shot was fired. He felt the bullet ball part his hair and he heard a cry of pain from behind him.

As he pushed himself up again, he hit La Ronde under his jaw with a clenched fist. The force of the blow sent La Ronde backwards, dropping his flintlock pistols and sliding over the big varnished table. Victor and Oliver dived away from the table as La Ronde crashed through the bay window, sending glass fragments in all directions. La Ronde vanished from sight.

Raymond spun around to see Francesca and Inspector Gibbins kneeling next to Joanna.

'How bad is it?' he asked.

'It's bad, she needs an ambulance.' In a softer voice the Inspector said, 'Journal is dead.' By the time the two plain clothes officers entered the room, Joanna had been moved to the settee and a call made for an ambulance.

'We heard two muffled shots!' one of the officers said as they looked around the room.

'Arrest those two men,' ordered Inspector Gibbins. The two officers produced handcuffs and proceeded to take Victor and Oliver into custody.

'Search them for weapons,' said Raymond, 'The big one, Oliver, may have a gun and the other one,

Victor, may have a Bowie knife,' The officers searched both men and found the Smith & Wesson and the knife as Raymond had predicted.

Before they were led out, and knowing that there was nothing he could do for Joanna, he asked, 'Victor, how did you and Oliver escape from custody, after being arrested at the Hell-Fire Club Caves?'

'We were taken to a hospital, thanks to you and, once we had been checked in and seen, we waited our chance and just walked out.'

'It was that easy,' said Raymond.

'Yes. Journal's man, Ginger, was shouting and swearing at the police officers so, while they were restraining him, we just walked out. Nobody asked any questions or challenged us. We were lost in the system.'

'Why the Bowie knife?' enquired Raymond.

'I've always wanted to be a knife fighter like Jim Bowie.'

'Would you give your life for your men and country?' asked Raymond.

'No,' Victor said indignantly, 'I only know of the famous sand bar fight where Bowie killed three men with his knife.'

'That brought him fame,' explained Raymond, 'but he chose to die at the Alamo with his friends, giving General Houston time to get his men into place to defend their country from General Santa Anna. Their battle cry was "Remember the Alamo!"

The two plain clothes officers began to lead Victor and Oliver out when Raymond remembered something, 'Victor, haven't you forgotten something?'

'No,' he answered.

'Where is it?' There was a pouch-like pocket on Victor's trousers. Raymond flipped it open and took out the silver knuckle duster with its two protruding points. He gave it to one of the officers.

'From the days when you wanted to be a vampire,' remarked Raymond. 'You are easily led, aren't you?'

'I know you don't think much of me, but Oliver and me, we are not murderers, we're just henchmen. Our job was to frighten, not to kill.' He soon realised that he was not going to get any sympathy from Raymond.

'You'll have to explain that in court.'

'How is the shoulder?' asked Victor, sarcastically.

'Occasionally it reminds me of you, but it will be much better, now that I know you'll both be in jail.' Then he added, 'How is your stomach?'

'I wish we'd never met in Austria,' Victor replied.

'So, do I,' remarked Raymond.

The two plain clothes officers were ready to leave with their prisoners, but just then the snow globe on the shelf above the fireplace caught the Inspector's eye. He picked it up and shook it, the tiny diamond chips sparkled as they swirled around the crystal.

'It's beautiful,' he said.

'Jo made it. It's the Herkimer quartz crystal that was used to replace the Snowflake Diamond. It's been renamed, The Crystal Mountain.'

'You say Miss Sommers made this?'

'Yes, it's unique. I did hear someone say, "there's not another like it."' Inspector Gibbins replaced it on the shelf and picked up the hand grenade. 'I will take charge of this.'

179

'Please do,' said Raymond. He crossed the room and picked up his shoulder bag, giving it to the Inspector he said. 'There is a gun and a knife inside. I took them from those two when I was on the Isles of Scilly.'

Inspector Gibbins placed the hand grenade very carefully inside the bag with the other weapons. Then Richard entered the room, 'Do you know that La Ronde is lying on your driveway?' He paused, 'He's dead.' Inspector Gibbins took the situation in hand, 'I'll have the bodies collected within the hour; and you have witnesses as to what took place here tonight.' He turned to Richard and said, 'Try not to let all this spoil your honeymoon.'

The Inspector spoke to Raymond before he left, 'I hope she will be alright and, don't forget, just a phone call, or come and visit me on the Islands and I will arrange things for you.' The Inspector smiled then he and his two officers left taking Oliver and Victor with them. No sooner had they left than an ambulance arrived and Joanna was taken to hospital, Rubin and Michael went with her, while Francesca and Richard stayed with Raymond at The Five Pines.

The Inspector was as good as his word; within the hour the bodies of Louis La Ronde and Captain James Journal were taken away. By the early hours of the morning The Five Pines was silent.

'That was a long day,' Francesca said, as she sat down on the settee next to Raymond, 'but a nice one. The wedding was wonderful, but now I am so worried about Jo.' They were all tired and they sat for a while in the quiet of the lounge, waiting for the phone to ring. The log fire was slowly going out, and as the flames began to fade Raymond said, 'Why don't you two go to bed? I will let you know if there is any word about Jo.'

When the log fire had burnt itself out, Raymond picked up the two flintlock pistols and placed them on the shelf above the fire place next to the snow globe, then retired to his bedroom. It was a comforting place for him. The walls were oak-panelled and the floor was covered with thick green carpet. There was a large bookshelf against one wall, full of well-thumbed classics. The windows looked out over the large gardens at the back of the house and gave such a beautiful aspect every morning, but all this was no comfort for his state of mind.

He tried to sleep, but all he could think of was Joanna. When he did sleep, it wasn't for long, and not a restful deep sleep. He heard the phone ring, It was about six o clock, he stirred himself to answer it before it woke Richard and Francesca, but they were already awake and joined him as he took the phone call. He didn't say much and at the end of the conversation he said, 'I am sorry, Rubin, thanks for letting me know.' He put the receiver down.

'What did they say?' asked Richard.

'It was Uncle Rubin,' he paused and breathed in deeply. 'He told me that Jo died during the night.' He felt an ice-cold shiver run down his spine. Hearing someone saying it, and saying it himself, were two different things.

'Rubin and your father will be back here about eleven. I am sorry Richard, Fran... I have to go somewhere...'

'Where do you have to go?' asked Richard.

'Just somewhere,' he said, and he left them. They watched him get into his Ferrari and leave the grounds of The Five Pines, the tyres throwing the little pebbles that made up the driveway into the air as he left. Though he was out of sight, they heard the sound of the Ferrari's tyres leaving rubber on the main road as he joined it.

'I hope he will be alright,' said Francesca.

'He is not thinking. He would never treat his Ferrari like that.'

'Where is he going?'

'I don't know and, at the moment, I don't think he does either.' Richard put his arm around his wife, 'Let's wait for your father and Rubin to come back, then we can decide what to do, together.'

Raymond travelled at great speed across Exmoor and it wasn't until he narrowly missed a wild deer that he began to slow down. The next few curves were taken too fast, and he knew it. He was only just able to stop the car from leaving the road on more than two occasions, more by instinct than anything else.

'Stop!' he shouted. He took his foot off the throttle and allowed the powerful sports car to slow down. He brought the Ferrari to a stop in a layby and turned the engine off.

'No!' he shouted. Then he grabbed the seat belts that were around him and pulled them sharply. They locked instantly. He pulled on them with all his might, shouting, 'No! No! No! No! NO!'

He took a few deep breaths, the rage within him slowly subsiding, but the sorrow he felt was so deep that he thought it would never leave him. He released the seat belts and they became movable again. Putting his hands over his face, he wiped the tears from his eyes.

'A new life,' he said. Then he started the engine, and the Ferrari moved gracefully away. Soon he was on the motorway and entering London. He wound his way through the London traffic and it was about eleven o clock when he parked the Ferrari in the car park of Scotland Yard. He left his car and boldly walked into the reception area where a uniformed officer asked if there was anything he could do for him.

'Yes please, I would like to see Inspector Gibbins.'

'I am sorry, sir, I think he has just left for the Isles of Scilly.' But as he said this, Inspector Gibbins came out of one of the offices, saying goodbye to his colleagues.

As he was passing through reception, Raymond called to him, 'Inspector, may I have a word with you?' The Inspector looked around to see Raymond.

'I am on my way back to the Isles of Scilly,' he said, 'but Mr. Spade, Ray, I will always have time to talk to you, come this way.' He took Raymond through a corridor and showed him into an office.

'What can I do for you?' he asked.

'Do you know that Jo died last night? It was one of the shots from La Ronde's flintlock pistols.'

'No, I didn't, I am sorry. That must be a great shock.'

'It is, but now I want to take you up on your offer.'

'You want to become a private investigator?'

'Yes, I want to help people who can't help themselves.'

'There are many of those, I could give you a list

of names right now. But if you are sure, I will start the process now. I need to see a few people, but I could have you ready for work very soon. Just one thing, what will you call your business and where will you work from?'

'I will work from home, The Five Pines, but I have no idea of a name.'

'I wish you well, and I will send your licence on to you when I have it and, if you don't mind, I will send you a list of names of people that need help now. In my position I can't help them, but you can, if you don't mind bending the law, just a bit.'

'Thank you, Inspector.'

'It is I who should thank you, I have been looking for someone like you for a long time. I am sorry about the circumstances that brought you to me, but I am sure that, between the two of us, we can make a difference. And now I really must go. I have a meeting that I must attend on St. Mary's. I have a Police helicopter waiting for me. I have no doubt we will meet again soon.' The two men shook hands and left Scotland Yard, one in a helicopter, the other in a Ferrari.

Raymond drove his sleek red sports car through the London traffic and out on to the motorway. It wasn't long before he was travelling across Exmoor. He knew he would have to attend Joanna's funeral and that would be very painful. These thoughts were in his mind as he drove along his driveway and parked the Ferrari next to the Bentley.

'I love you, Jo, truly I do,' he said. Then he switched off the engine and went into the house. He made his way to the kitchen as that was where he could hear voices. He entered to see Richard,

Francesca, Rubin and Michael. Richard greeted him, 'Ray! I am glad to see you! It gave us a bit of a fright, seeing the Ferrari leave as fast as it did.'

'Yes, sorry about that, I was upset, unbalanced, you might even say temporarily insane, but I am alright now. How are all of you?'

There was a silence, then Rubin broke the tense atmosphere. 'Would you like some coffee, my boy?'

'Yes, please.'

Francesca poured a cup of black coffee.

Rubin spoke again, 'I will talk to the Vicar and make some arrangements. We might as well get on and do what has to be done.' He looked at his brother, his niece and at his two friends.

'Yes,' added Michael, 'Jo wouldn't want us to stop doing what must be done.'

The next few days passed in a blur of the necessary officialdom accompanying a death and Jo's funeral was arranged and attended by her friends and family. It was a difficult time for her father and uncle, but they did have each other and they planned to live in Michael's cottage, two retired gentlemen. Francesca had Richard to help her, and the plans went ahead for them to live in Rubin's cottage, although they stayed with Raymond at The Five Pines for the moment.

Raymond attended the funeral. He did what was expected of him and showed no emotions. He couldn't describe what he was feeling and felt fortunate that Joanna had known his feelings for her. He would hold on to that in the difficult days ahead.

The days continued to pass and Raymond was amazed that life went on, but it did. Rubin and Michael had moved out, and the sale of Rubin's house in York was completed. Richard and Francesca stayed at The Five Pines with Raymond and Richard had returned to work with Sam and the safety team. But now it was time for them to take their long overdue honeymoon.

They were sitting at the breakfast table when Richard announced, 'I have had an idea. I have mentioned it to Sam and he said I could take the time and the Porsche…'

Francesca interrupted. 'What idea?'

'Taking our honeymoon. I thought we should go to Scotland.'

'That is a good idea,' remarked Raymond, 'I have spent a few holidays there. Such a beautiful place, you might even get someone who will serve you haggis and a very fine single malt,'

'I have never tasted haggis, but I have tasted a good malt whisky.' Richard waited for Francesca to say something. She looked deep in thought, then she said, 'Yes, I would like to go to Scotland,' then a smile came to her face, 'we must try and get a sighting of Nessie.'

'And a photograph,' added Richard.

The atmosphere around the breakfast table was lighter than it had been since Joanna's funeral. Even Raymond was being involved in the planning of the honeymoon. There were lots of phone calls to make and packing to do and, by late afternoon, almost everything was arranged. Richard and Francesca planned to leave the following morning. The day had turned out to be a very hectic one, but now they were relaxing in the lounge.

Raymond was saying, 'I have driven that road from Fort William to Inverness and I would bet that everyone on that road would not be able to pass without looking for the monster.'

'Come on, Ray, her name is Nessie,' said Francesca.

'How do you know it's a she?'

'She has never been caught,' she smiled.

They talked late into the night and it almost felt like it used to. Eventually Richard and Francesca retired to their room and Raymond checked that all the doors and windows were locked, and then retired to his bedroom.

It was quite late in the morning when Raymond walked into the kitchen. He had seen the travel bags that were packed and ready to be taken to the car. Francesca presented him with a cup of coffee and Richard greeted him with, 'Good morning, we are almost ready to leave. We have booked a few days in a little inn on the shores of Loch Ness.'

'I wish you lots of luck and I hope you get a sighting.'

'If we get a sighting, we will get a photograph,' Richard said happily. Then he added, 'Will you be ok here on your own?'

'I will be just fine, thanks for asking, Richard,' Raymond accompanied them to the cars. 'Have a good time,' he said.

'We will,' came the reply. Raymond watched as the Porsche wound its way through the grounds of The Five Pines and lost sight of it as it took Richard and Francesca on another adventure.

As he turned to go back into the house, he noticed a white Ford Lotus sports car enter the grounds. It accelerated along the driveway and slid to a stop not far from where he was standing. The driver rose from the driver's seat and jump over the door. She was dressed in blue jeans and denim jacket. She walked boldly to where he was standing.

'Are you Raymond Spade?'

'Yes, I am.' He looked into her blue eyes and watched her shoulder length blond hair moving in the breeze.

'Inspector Gibbins sent me to you. He said you can help me. Is this The Five Pines?'

'Yes, it is.'

'Are you an investigator?'

He paused before answering.

'Yes... yes, I am, but before you ask any more questions, may I ask your name?'

'Josephine.'

'Josephine who?' he asked.

'Ryder, Josephine Ryder, you can call me Jo.'

Raymond felt a lump in his throat. This wasn't the Jo he knew, but there was a remarkable resemblance. He cleared his throat and struggled to say, 'You can call me Ray. Come in.' His emotions subsided a little and he finished his sentence, 'Have some coffee and tell me what brings you here.'

They entered The Five Pines together. Raymond closed the big oak front door. This felt better, not right, but better. He showed Josephine into the kitchen, poured two cups of coffee, then he led her up the stairs to the lounge. They placed the coffee cups on the large table and looked out through the bay window at the drive way below and the gardens.

'How can I help you, Jo?' he asked. She produced a brown envelope from inside her denim jacket and placed it on the table. His name was written on it.

'It's from my father,' she said. Raymond picked it up and opened it.

'A private investigator's licence.' He paused for a moment, 'A Ray of Hope'. Is your father Inspector Gibbins?'

'Yes,' she replied.

'But you said your name was Ryder.'

'That's right, Josephine Ryder, Mrs.'

Raymond picked up his cup and drank some coffee. He thought for a moment and then asked, 'Who gave my business a name?'

'I did,' she answered. 'When he told me about you, and how you are going to try to help those who can't help themselves, I thought you would be a real ray of hope.'

He smiled, it had been a long time since his smile had been spontaneous. He asked again, 'How can I help you, Jo?'

'My father thinks very highly of you. He said if anyone can help me, it would be you. My husband, Jonathon Ryder, is a freelance journalist and photographer. He was investigating the Legend of the Wizard of the Edge. There are several local legends about Alderley Edge, the Wizard of the Edge being the most famous. He took some time off for our wedding and, when our wedding day arrived, it was wonderful. However, after a day or two he returned to the investigation at Alderley Edge, and we decided to take our honeymoon when he was finished. Now he is missing. He has not been seen for a week. I tried to explain the situation to my father, but he said there were no tangible leads and, though he would do what he could, it would be difficult to start a police investigation into a legend. Do you know just how big the missing persons' list is?'

'No, I haven't needed to check it.'

'It's big,' her voice softened, 'so he sent me to you.'

Raymond finished the last of his coffee and said, 'I will look into it, I am going to need some time to observe the activities at Alderley Edge.'

Her hand reached out to his, she only touched his fingers, 'Be careful, Ray. People get killed there.' She finished her coffee and announced that it was time for her to leave. She gave Raymond a contact number and left the table. Raymond followed her to the door but, as she passed the fireplace, she saw the two guns and the snow globe on the shelf.

'May I?' she asked as she picked up one of the guns. She looked at it carefully.

'The precious gems alone must be worth a fortune.'

'Yes, they are.'

'Did they cost a lot?'

'The cost was great and the price was too high, much more than I was willing to pay.' He hesitated. 'They are evidence in a double murder. I am expecting someone from forensics to collect them any time now.'

She replaced the gun on the shelf and they left the lounge. Raymond accompanied her to her car. She opened the driver's door of the sleek Ford Lotus and sat in the driver's seat.

'I will contact you in a day or so. Try not to worry. One way or another I will find Jonathon for you.'

'Thank you,' she answered as she started the engine, 'I'll wait to hear from you.' Then she asked inquisitively, 'Ray, who did the jewel encrusted guns belong to?'

'That's a closed case,' he answered. 'They

belonged to Louis La Ronde, known as the man with the flintlock pistols, now deceased.'

Lightning Source UK Ltd.
Milton Keynes UK
UKHW010613210719
346476UK00001B/134/P

9 781911 265948